First Face North
The Truth Seeker's Wayfinder
Rob McPhillips

Published by Ruth Layton

What Readers Say

I just don't think I can attempt to write all the things I am thinking about right now. I am being literally bombarded with insights… I am just floored tonight. I was not expecting that… I was hopeful, yes. But this is truly awesome, amazing, inspiring stuff!

STELLA

When I happened upon your ebook, I was crippled by anxieties and felt that life was too difficult to overcome. I remember being drawn to a line that read "…life is just so simple." What followed were quite brilliant analytical essays about the processes of life and the tools necessary to benefit from these processes and create your own life experience. I was mesmerised. The book outlined a belief system that belonged to me from a very young age, but one that I had lost sight of over time. I could not recommend this book highly enough because it is filled with page after page of home truths, humbly written in honesty by a guy looking to better understand the world around us.

OSBOURNE

From the time I read about First Face North, it has inspired me and educated me on how to be happy (and) cope with and overcome my anxieties in life. It not only changed my life but what I have learned from this has been shared also with my friends who are experiencing the same.

ROLLY

I don't remember now the exact details of the book, (I read it three years ago), but I do remember how I felt. The first thing I remember was being really impressed by the depth of your understanding of seemingly complex matters and how effectively you were able to convey it. It's the clarity your words provide that is hard to find with other books. The insights in the book are in a league of their own, as we say here in the states. I wrote you a comment at the time that said it was one of the best I'd read ever and recommended then you publish it. I feel the same today.

BRIAN

I wanted to let you know that I have not finished your book — contrary to the norm I am not rushing to finish it. I want to savor it and to reinforce the themes that are helping me increase the amount of happiness I am perceiving. There are so many nuggets in your book. Many of which I have heard before but for some reason they are sinking in better this time. I think it may have to do with the way you write.

DOUG

I am indeed grateful and feel very inspired after I read your e-book. I was at my lowest point at that time when I chanced upon to see your site and read your e-book. I recall the feeling of having clarity showered upon me while and after I have read your e-book. It was literally one of those e-books I'd recommend to anyone to read to have that sense of clarity and be inspired to move on with their life despite all the obstacles they have.

MAGGIE

I would say that your book was one of my key building blocks in understanding the science of happiness. What differentiated your book was its simplicity...

SIVA

Preface

I first came to Rob's book through an overwhelming desire for peace during a time of extreme emotional pain. I searched the net, hoping to find help, and after some months I found this book. I printed it out and began to read it every Friday night — my worst time after a busy week at work and the start of what then seemed to be an endless weekend alone, something I now welcome. At first it was the stories that held me, and I read them over and over again; I gradually read and began to understand the power of Rob's words, use the web site, and speak to him regularly on the phone. Following this, I began a wonderful journey which still continues and will do so throughout life: reading and spending time with spiritual teachers of many kinds — including friends, pets and nature — on a daily basis.

It is perhaps serendipity that, as I write this three years later, I am in a similar emotional situation. The shift in my way of being that began with this book has brought me to a place which is calmer, more peaceful, and although I feel the emotion very powerfully — it is not who I am at my core — it is as though I am stepping back and looking at it sitting on a distant hilltop. I can even smile at the situation now. This does not mean I have closed down or I don't care — rather, that I have more space to respond with love, to be more authentically my true self.

Through these experiences and the profound increased happiness in my daily existence, I feel motivated to bring this book to as many people as possible. I look back and realise I had moments much earlier in life when I wanted to change, but then another external factor would absorb me which at the time seemed so important—and the years passed. It now seems complete madness that anything could seem more important than internal peace.

This beautiful book is accessible to everyone; the stories can be read to and by children and adults, told at dinner parties or even business meetings, it can be picked up and read for 5 minutes or for a whole day. Maybe just look at the images, maybe just pick it up and hold it sometimes; all I can say is enjoy. It will start or accelerate an internal change in you, and this is the way—the only way—to change the external world: a truthful reflection of our collective being.

RUTH LAYTON

More than just a read. Join in online
and make it a personal journey.

www.firstfacenorth.com

Introduction

Deep underneath our superficial differences and idiosyncrasies, we all want the same thing. We all want peace, love, happiness, and a sense of security. Yet it is in the details of what these look like and how we achieve them that cause our conflicts.

Deep down, every parent wants the best for their child… yet parents frequently argue over what is best and how to achieve it. Leaders want the best for their nation or organisation… yet there is always conflict about what is best and how to go about it.

At the core, we share the same wants and needs. Yet we keep this core hidden from much of the world, showing instead our social face — how we want the world to see us.

So there becomes a separation of worlds, the truth of what we really want and the surface thoughts, words, and actions that meet the world we live in. In part this is caused by the nature of language and its vague representation of what we mean. Take a vague concept like happiness, and the word means completely different things to different people. However, it is also clouded in our own lack of honesty or self-awareness.

For example, we may really want to feel respected and acknowledged, but this may surface in the world as wanting Ferraris and Jimmy Choos. The power of brands is in the way they portray what we aspire to. And we aspire to what we believe will meet our core needs.

It is in the tangled web of how our core wants and needs get translated into the surface that we become lost and confused. We lose ourselves and then we lose our way.

We lose ourselves in the flow of demands and pressures from the world. Yet our core desires remain, and every emotion we feel is generated as a direct response as to how well we are meeting that need.

Throughout history people have tried to eliminate desires that their culture thought were wrong. Yet the truth is, if you want something, deep down there's a valid reason why. You cannot eliminate the desire. You just need to understand it in its true form. No desire is evil at its core, but many get perverted and distorted into something very ugly as they reach the surface.

We lose our way when we are overpowered by emotional attachment to a certain outcome. Blinded by lust, greed, or fear, we become so obsessed and fixated on our desire that we lose sight of firstly: what we truly want; and secondly: the path to getting it.

My mission in life over the last three decades has been to help Truth Seekers strip away the web of confusion to understand what they truly want and then to recognise the path to it.

People often confuse truth with honesty. Yet we may speak honestly, but if we are misguided or have an incomplete understanding, we still are not speaking truth.

Truth is what is at the core that motivates people despite what they say or do. Willpower and discipline can stem the flow for so long, but eventually core drives burst through. It is the truth of what is at the core that determines how a relationship, career, or business will work out. Truth is the blueprint that underpins all of our personal, economic, and social changes.

Understanding the truth of a situation cuts out unnecessary emotional suffering and turmoil and saves wasted efforts —chasing smoke and mirrors.

You see, the world that you see about you, the situations you are faced with, and even the people around you are made up of hard and soft landscapes. What I mean by this is that there is the hard landscape that you can't change, the core desires, and the natural world. You can't change what you truly are and you can't change things like gravity.

However the soft landscape is made up of extensions of the hard landscape. Interpretations and stories that we think best represent what we feel and understand. So we think we want the promotion, but really we want recognition or security. We think we understand why the sun rises and sets, yet so, too, did our ancestors a thousand years before Copernicus explained the stationary nature of the sun.

The things that you want in the social world are interpretations of your core desire. And so these can be re-interpreted and refined. Our emotional pain comes from wanting to change what cannot be changed — the core wants and natural laws — to maintain our whims and social wants.

To be too attached to anything in the soft landscapes is akin to dancing on a volcano. People can and do succeed hugely without harmonising with truth. They can trick the market, the girl, and the world — though the tectonic plates of truth will move, and as they do, you are likely to find your world crashing around you... unless you have been guided by the deeper truth.

It IS Your Fault

Life is not democratic. It doesn't operate on any basis of fairness that people typically expect or recognise. The starting circumstances of our life are beyond our control, a complete accident of birth.

Some of us are born into prosperous, loving families in countries with lots of opportunities. Others are born in barren lands and/or with families that neglect or abuse them. Some are gifted with brains, beauty, and balance. Others seem to have been short-changed in almost all departments.

If our happiness is dependent on what we have, rather than our attitude to what we have, then we have a God who plays very cruel tricks. I cannot believe that we have a world that contains such a perfectly coordinated ecosystem with such intricately interlinked systems and structures that allows life to play out in many constantly evolving forms — yet through its design, it deliberately picks on some.

I believe instead, that the unfairness of the world is deliberately designed to provide a lavish smorgasbord of opportunities for inner evolution. It is not progress in the outer world that counts — though the two are not at odds, as some would have it — but the development of an increasingly rich and refined inner landscape.

This inner growth is not a matter of linear development, encouraging superiority and smugness as some "spiritually" inclined folk would have it. It is the continual opportunity to grow in multiple directions from wherever you might be at a given moment to where will make you feel more connected, secure, and bring you a more vivid and joyful experience of life.

While your start in life is out of your control, where you go from there is determined by the choices you make. It matters not what you've done in the past. The simple choice in every minute is to be happier or more frustrated. The choice is yours and yours alone to make.

Lots of well-meaning but misguided people will try to take this choice away from people in the belief that they know best.

"It's not your fault," they say, "the system/your parents failed you". The fact is that if you are dependent on anyone else for you to be happier, than you're screwed. When you're lost and frustrated, it sucks to feel like it's your fault. You want to blame something else — anyone other than you — so that you don't feel like a screw-up. But the real problem is your focus.

Let me explain. You see, the real problem is you were looking back at what you can't change instead of ahead to what you can change. And in using excuses as a Band-Aid to make you feel better about what's gone, you've given away your ability to change things in the future.

I know that what's happened in your life to upset you probably wasn't fair or right and you probably do have every reason to feel aggrieved, but the critical question to ask yourself is:

Do I want to be happy or right?

The experience of life is not determined by what's around you, but by whether you are moving in the direction of what you want or away from it. It is in how successfully you meet the challenge of relating to life.

It is this sense of responsibility that is the core determinant of whether you seek truth or not. Truth Seekers aim to align with Life, rather than the temporal and transient beliefs of their culture. In doing so, they build on sound foundations rather than on a house of cards that will at any moment collapse. And so they can build layer on layer to make every day better than the last.

It is not a case of learning certain practices or knowledge, though this is a step along the way for some people. It is more about the spirit with which you tackle the problems and challenges along the way.

That spirit of investigating what is truth and orientating ourselves to it starts with finding our bearings, our personal North. Throughout this book are 34 tweaks and reinterpretations I have made to my soft landscapes and shared with others who also found them useful. None of this is necessarily revolutionary; it doesn't need to be. There is only one true way to happiness… to find and align with truth… yet this is expressed in a million different ways. So, too, is this book another expression.

34 Ideas For Truth
Seekers To Consider

34 Accompanying Short Stories

❊ *North and South identify the opposite poles and the axis of rotation of the Earth. North is the point at which we begin the journey, the point from which we go ahead, turn left, right or around — it's where we start.*

The location of the Sun, the time of day, the stars in the night sky, the weather, the lay of the land, the behaviour of plants and animals and the rocks that form Earth help us understand where we are in the world.

Observation and understanding permit self-orientation. In a physical or emotional landscape, navigation is made simpler by our ability to appreciate the journey.

✻ *The Sun's diameter is 1,391,000 km,*
which is 109 times as big as the
Earth and over 400 times as big
as the Moon.

Sun 1,391,940 km
Earth 12,742 km
Moon 3,476 km

THINGS JUST ARE

If you understand, things are just as they are; if you do not understand, things are just as they are.

Zen Proverb

I.

Understand the True Nature of Life

Life is so, so simple. There can be nothing simpler to understand. Yet so many people struggle. Walk into any major bookshop and you'll find hundreds of books promising you eternal bliss... wonderful relationships, and all the success you can handle.

Yet very few people are able to use this information. More people still struggle with these issues than don't—even when they've read the books. So then they go read more books. Still, they don't get it. Now they're really frustrated, and so they believe life must be incredibly complex.

It isn't.

Here's the secret to life. Don't rush through this; it is really important.

> If you find something difficult to understand intellectually... it's because you don't want to accept it emotionally.

> If you accept it emotionally... intellectually, it's simple.

What happens is that when we come across something that challenges a belief that we want to hold onto, we complicate it by trying to make it fit around the thing we want to hold onto. It doesn't work. So then we keep looking and making the solution ever more complex.

For instance, when people want to lose weight, they need to eat less calories than they burn. Simple as that. Either eat less or burn up more. Typically, though, dieters want to continue to eat in much the same way as they have. And so they look not for the simple solution, but for the magic solution that tells them they can still eat their favourite chocolate cake, have a drink, and yet miraculously still lose weight.

Life is an infinitely layered experience. Different people operate on different layers, and so they see the same thing in very different ways. Neither is necessarily wrong. If you could only see the front part of an elephant and thought that was all there was, and I only the back, we'd both think that we were experiencing different things. But we're not. It takes a more distanced perspective to see all of the elephant. With all three views, you are able to take the close ups to add detail to the overall.

In much the same way, once you understand life on different levels, you are better equipped to enjoy it more. Generally people read books like this to learn what they need to do to be happy. Then they think they mustn't be doing it right if it doesn't work. The truth is; there isn't anything you have to do to be happy. You've just got to stop the things you're doing now that make you unhappy. In this book, we are going to cover the almost universal mistakes that cause people to squander their energy, enthusiasm, and happiness. As you go through the book, remember:

If you find something difficult to understand intellectually...

This book looks at life on a deeper level than many people are used to. That's because the most profound and lasting change is at the core of what you are, which underlies the more obvious emotions and behaviours.

Sometimes people seem to have a resistance to getting deep. This is because emotions are stronger here. If you feel a strong emotion, it means you are reading, thinking, or talking about something that is important to you. The stronger the emotion, the more important to you it is. This means that once you get to the root of the cause, the more powerful the emotion, the bigger the change. And so the happier you will feel.

Many people read books like this and want practical steps to get on with. I have put some exercises on the accompanying members' area website, which you can find at:
www.firstfacenorth.com

They are not the definitive principles or even necessary steps. They are tools that can help you to integrate the principles into your everyday life, which is going to be different from everyone else's. Sometimes people get hooked on the tools and miss that they are just a vehicle to get you to your destination. My aim in everything that I do is to challenge your thinking so that in the process of deciding between two or more choices, you get the opportunity to choose the best and truest version.

Of course you can make changes through the practical steps, and they can help you solve the problems that are facing you. But if you use techniques to solve problems without changing the source of problems, they just keep coming back in different forms.

The path ahead is simple, easier than the path you took to get here. If it isn't, work out what emotional attachment is the obstacle.

Everything in life is simple... you just need to grasp the basics. When I was seventeen or eighteen, I used to go to boxing training. There was one thing that marked out the best boxers. Barring exceptional natural ability, the best were those who'd been boxing for the longest time. It takes seven or eight years for a boxer to reach his peak.

Because when your head is swimming—when you don't know who you are or where you are—the experienced boxers protected themselves and fought their way out to survive and recover. The moves and strategies were so ingrained into them that they just became a natural response. The others, when they got disorientated, lost the ability to move and so never recovered.

In the same way, the difference between a black belt martial artist and a novice is that the black belt knows many variations of the same few basic techniques. The successful business carries out the basic steps more effectively and consistently than the less successful.

Get the basics right and the rest will come easily. If you don't get them right, nothing else can work effectively.

The root of our problems is that most of our knowledge about life has been passed down from generation to generation. However, that knowledge was based on what our ancestors understood about life. Today, with scientific discoveries and advancements in our understandings, this knowledge is out of date. So the basic beliefs we have that underlie everything we do... are preventing us from being anywhere near as effective and happy as we could be.

Yet because we get so caught up in life, we don't consciously realise these misunderstandings. And as they underpin all our thoughts and actions, our relationships, and our businesses, it makes life so much harder and less enjoyable than it could be.

Life is like a great experimental laboratory. If our beliefs are flawed, acting on them feels bad. If we keep on doing it, but try harder... we'll feel even worse. The harder we try, the worse it gets. If what we think is true, we feel good.

For most people today, in at least some areas, life doesn't feel good. This is because conventional wisdom is flawed.

It's based on outdated ideas and beliefs.

It doesn't work.

The harder we try, the worse it feels. The solutions to the problems our world faces are not going to come through legislation or indoctrination. The problems are not a matter of finding the right way to control and contain people. They are merely a reflection of what we believe.

When we as individuals can get over the arrogant assumption that we are here to fix the world and everyone in it, the world will show us what works and what doesn't.

Most people have been taught to think of our planet as a giant doll's house. And ourselves as a doll placed in there. By this I mean that we look out on the world. We see that it was here and seemed complete long before we were here. And we know it will go on without us. So in that sense, the world looks far more solid and important than us.

Yet just the law of gravity shows us that a simple movement can have enormous consequences. Everything is affected by you and affects everything else in the universe.

The flapping of a single butterfly's wing today produces a tiny change in the state of the atmosphere. Over a period of time, what the atmosphere actually does diverges from what it would have done. So, in a month's time, a tornado that would have devastated the Indonesian coast doesn't happen. Or maybe one that wasn't going to happen, does.

Ian Stewart, Does God Play Dice?
The Mathematics of Chaos, pg. 141

A smile that is meaningless to you may change entirely what another may do, causing dramatic changes to the rest of the world. Every action you make is significant.

Yet as we look on the world without realising this, we often feel as if we are insignificant or unneeded. If things don't go so well, we look out at the doll's house and we say, "Oh well, that can't move. It must be me that doesn't fit. Maybe they put me in the wrong room. I need to find the place where I fit in."

That's where it all starts to go wrong. You cannot bend to fit into the doll house. It is in your trying to fit in where life goes astray.

The picture of Earth as a doll's house is false. All of life is in relation to you. Every action of yours causes a reaction in the world. I don't say this to make you feel good. It's a rule of gravity.

You are an integrated part of this planet travelling 16,000 miles per hour through the universe. At no moment is anything around you static. We are all hurtling through life, all bound one to the other.

You cannot get off this ride, but you can learn to steer it and travel without getting motion sickness.

To do this, you first need to stand up and decide to take control of your life. The first principle to ingrain into yourself is an understanding that everything in life is in relation to you. You are the hub, everyone and everything else are the spokes. It doesn't matter what they did to you, what twist of fate happened 50,000 miles back. It's all about you. You can spend the next decade whinging and complaining about how hard life is, or you can learn the lessons life shows you and start to steer your life.

The source of all pain and misery come down to one fundamental mistake.

Pain or misery is the clashing of what life is with what you think life should be.

Give up the need to have life be exactly how you think it should, and you need never feel frustration and anger again. None of us have a deep enough knowledge to have the first idea what would be best for ourselves—let alone anyone else or the world in general.

We misunderstand what life is, how it works, and what its purpose is. The more firmly that we believe in this misunderstanding, the more pain and misery we create. Give up control—which you've never really had anyway—and you can direct everything.

Life is so much vaster, has so many more possibilities and so much more flexibility than we realise. The way we experience life is like the way we listen to the radio. We tune in to a specific wavelength. This lets us hear one station clearly, but cuts out other stations.

In any given situation we have hundreds of choices. By focusing only on our current wavelength, we miss other possibilities and choices. Therefore, we trap ourselves. Then we think *I have no choice,* or *I have only A and B to choose between.* And so we feel frustrated, trapped—with little, if any, power. This creates frustration, anger, despair, and misery.

Once you can truly recognise and appreciate the beauty and perfection of life, you can change your focus, just as we change radio stations. Then life becomes far simpler and more exciting.

Once our problems were relatively simple to solve. We needed food and shelter. These were there already, we just had to find a way to harvest them. Today our problems are so complex that most people do not even understand them.

Our planet faces destruction from global warming and weapons of mass destruction. Soil erosion means that our food has minimal if any nutritional value. Superbugs and super viruses threaten us almost every flu season.

These threats have all been created by our society in the last few decades. Of course we did not intend for these effects. But when we act in the world without appreciating the order of nature, believing that we need to fix it, we end up stumbling from one disaster to another.

And what is true of us as a society is also true of us as individuals. As individuals, we go through life trying to help others, or even ourselves, believing we and they need fixing, thinking that we — or anyone else — can see enough to know the right path for others.

No-one is broken or needs fixing. Nature is perfect. When we understand this, we can get over the need to make everyone else think and act as we do. And then we can begin to appreciate others for the gifts and talents they can share with us. Then, instead of straining to fit into regulation shapes, we can all fit together like one huge jigsaw.

The key to life is to fall in love with it. To start to treat it as a big investigative game. You can begin to create order out of the chaos of life. And learn the universal laws and principles that govern life.

With this approach, each day you'll learn more about yourself and life. You'll begin to understand why things happened and see more options. Then you'll feel more secure and in control of your life.

It all starts when you stop calling life a bitch and cursing your luck.

You can't change anything while you're hitting out at the world.

But when you love life... life starts to love you.

Remember when you first fell in love. You wanted to know all about that person.

- All about their past.
- All about what they were thinking.
- All about what their hopes and dreams were.

You woke up in the morning and just gazed at your lover, appreciating their inner and outer beauty.

Why do you think life should be any different?

To feel the same way about life, you have to stop treating it like the adverts before the main feature. You know, the way you "kill time" while waiting for what you really want. Start:

- Courting life.
- Getting curious and fascinated by the beauty of life.
- Enjoying the romance and sheer adventure of being alive.

Forget the myths of romance and chemistry. Study after study shows that it is familiarity that is most influential in deciding whom we fall in love with. We love what we know. What we do not know, we fear.

Have you ever wondered what determines beauty? Psychologists have investigated and at least part of it has to do with familiarity.

If you take a hundred faces and morph them into one blended face, that face will be more attractive than fifty morphed faces. And fifty morphed faces will be judged more attractive than twenty five, and so on.

It seems that unusual features are considered ugly, whereas beauty is judged to be common or symmetrical features. It reflects back what the observer sees and understands. The more we know about something, the more we like it.

People who don't like each other often become friends if they are put in a situation where they have to spend a lot of time together.

Why?

Because we don't like what we don't understand. At the basest level, we see this in prejudice against someone of a different race, creed, or even organisation. Once we learn and understand why someone thinks and acts differently, we can appreciate them—even if we still disagree with their conclusions.

Art, sport, or a type of music we know nothing about can seem so boring… but once we learn a little we can get hooked.

What does any of this have to do with you falling in love with life?

Falling in love with life is about paying attention and understanding it. It's about being fascinated with the process of life and treating it as a lover who you are endlessly interested in, rather than viewing it as the way to get the stuff you think you want.

Once you get this mindset, the path forward is clear.

☀ *To make one complete 24-hour revolution, the Earth spins anticlockwise on an oscillating axis of 23.5°, rotating 15° every hour. Each part of the world experiences, in turn: dawn, day, night and dusk as the sun comes in and out of view.*

I'LL BE HAPPY WHEN...

We convince ourselves that life will be better after we get married, have a baby, then another.

Then we are frustrated that the kids aren't old enough, and we'll be more content when they are.

After that, we're frustrated that we have teenagers to deal with. We will certainly be happy when they are out of that stage.

We tell ourselves that our life will be complete when our spouse gets his or her act together, when we get a nicer car, are able to go on a nice vacation, when we retire.

The truth is, there's no better time to be happy than right now.

If not now, when?

Your life will always be filled with challenges.

It's best to admit this to yourself and decide to be happy anyway.

One of my favorite quotes comes from Alfred D Souza. He said, "For a long time it had seemed to me that life was about to begin —real life. But there was always some obstacle in the way, something to be gotten through first, some unfinished business, time still to be served, or a debt to be paid. Then life would begin. At last it dawned on me that these obstacles were my life."

This perspective has helped me to see that there is no way to happiness. Happiness is the way.

So, treasure every moment that you have and treasure it more because you shared it with someone special, special enough to spend your time… and remember that time waits for no one.

So, stop waiting until you finish school,
until you go back to school,
until you lose ten pounds,
until you gain ten pounds,
until you have kids,

until your kids leave the house,
until you start work,
until you retire,
until you get married,
until you get divorced,
until Friday night, until Sunday morning,
until you get a new car or home,
until your car or home is paid off,
until spring,
until summer,
until fall,
until winter,
until you are off welfare,
until the first or fifteenth,
until your song comes on,
until you've had a drink,
until you've sobered up,
until you die,

until you are born again to decide that there is no better time than right now to be happy.

Happiness is a journey, not a destination.

UNTIL YOU GET WHERE YOU'RE GOING...

2.

Come to a Deeper Understanding of Happiness

Really all there is... is life. It's just a continuous, flowing experience. But because we impose our own mental structures to break it down and categorise it, we make up all these different labels for different experiences.

Trying to categorise and make sense of what are unique experiences takes up an enormous amount of energy.

If you can free yourself from this — in other words if you can think outside of the cultural box — you have a great deal more mental energy to enjoy life as it comes.

For centuries, people have agonised over what love and happiness are.

They are the uninhibited experience of life. You cannot understand them through words. You can only understand them through experience.

Love and happiness are the same feeling from different perspectives.

Happiness is the experience of loving life. Being happy is being in love with that momentary experience.

And love is looking at someone or even something and seeing the absolute best of him/her/it. Love is happiness with what you see.

So love and happiness really are the same thing, just expressed differently.

Yet people think of happiness, or love, as a rare, limited experience. They worry that it may never pass by them again — believing it is something that happens to them, rather than a state they create themselves.

When they experience it they are so focused on keeping it that they cannot fully enjoy it. They think that if they can trap it, and cage it, they can keep it forever.

But life is change. The river of life is the constant and continual evolutionary force of change. Without continual cellular renewal, every living thing decays. As the experience of happiness becomes trapped, it loses its nourishment. And so it decays. So what once was the picture of beauty and joy is now a decaying, rotting ugliness. Not because of the cruelty of life, but because the source of the beauty (the life force) got cut off.

There is no puppet master manipulating the world to antagonise or test you. There is only yourself.

Do you let yourself enjoy the beauty of the world?

Or do you try to force it to fit in with your expectations and demands and end up holding a decrepit corpse of life?

Happiness or love cannot be achieved or orchestrated. It can only be enjoyed. Once you try to force or manipulate life to fit in with your beliefs, you distort it.

Just as if a tree is allowed to grow, it will grow into a thing of beauty and strength. If its light is cut off, if its way is blocked, it will grow distorted. It will always grow, either in beauty or ugliness. It's the same with your life. You either trust in life or distort it.

It always feels better to love than to hate.

We prefer to see beauty than ugliness.

It feels better to praise and appreciate than to criticise and blame.

So the more of your life you spend praising and appreciating beauty... the more of your life you will love.

But what if what you see is not beautiful?

If what you see is not beautiful, it is because you are not looking deeply enough to see the beauty.

Crumbs from a cake look messy, but the full cake is beautiful. Parts of life look messy only because we don't see the bigger picture. We often look through blinkers at what is in front of us, seeing only the crumbs.

Yet behind what you observe, there are layers and layers of life to see. Find the thing to appreciate and choose to put your focus there, and life will seem beautiful.

❊ *Commonly known as sunrise and sunset, the hours that surround these events are the most reliable reference for which we can easily calculate which way is North.*

Over the sea the reflection of the Sun when low in the sky forms a shimmering path. At 90° from this path we know we face the top of our planet, North. As the Sun rises its point of origin and destination become less obvious.

THE ONE

Many years ago, in a time of great war and consternation, there was a monastery which had fallen upon hard times.

There were few monks left, and they tended to squabble amongst themselves. Everyone was convinced their path was the right path, and the peaceful ways of the past seemed little more than a dream.

In a last-ditch attempt to save the monastery, the abbot went to seek the wisdom of an old rabbi who was reputed to have great insight and wisdom into the ways of men.

When the abbot told the rabbi of the situation, the rabbi shook his head with great concern.

Source Unknown

"It is imperative that you find a way to resolve this situation before it is too late," said the rabbi. "For what you do not realise is that among you is the One who will deliver us all from fear into love."

The abbot asked who among them was the One, but the rabbi would tell him no more. On the way back to the monastery, he wondered who the One could be. *I'll bet it's Brother Arthur,* he thought to himself. *He is kind and good. Or perhaps it is Brother Thomas—he is young but already shows great wisdom. Or could it be… no… I mustn't even consider that it might be me!*

On his return, the abbot shared the news with the monks. While they were startled, there was a ring of truth to what the abbot had said. The One was amongst them!

As they contemplated which of them it might be, the monks began to treat one another with a very special reverence and respect. After all, someone among them might really be the One. And, on the off chance that each monk himself might be the One, they began to treat themselves with extraordinary respect and reverence, as well.

As time went by, the monks developed a gentle, loving quality about them which was hard to quantify but easy to notice. They lived respectfully, in harmony with themselves and nature.

An aura of respect and reverence seemed to radiate out from them and permeate the atmosphere. There was something strangely attractive, even compelling about it.

Occasional visitors found themselves deeply moved by the life of these monks. Before long, people were coming from far and wide to be nourished by the life of the monks, and young men were asking to become a part of their community. Within a few short years, the monastery had once again become a thriving order—a vibrant centre of light and spirituality in the world.

3.
Recognise the Path
to True Happiness

When people find out that I spend my time writing and speaking to people about happiness, they ask one question.

"So what is the secret? What does it take to be happy?"

They think there is some secret formula. That if they had enough money, enough love, enough *things*, they would automatically be happy.

The way that they speak of happiness and ask the question indicates that happiness isn't something they have considered deeply. They haven't considered it deeply, because they believe that there are so many other things they have to do first before they can be happy.

But because they aren't happy, life is so much harder than it needs to be. When happiness is your first priority, everything else comes easily. In a car, oil smoothes the way for everything else. It lubricates the engine and protects it from friction that would cause damage.

Happiness works in the same way for our lives. It makes our relationships, our work, and everything else in our lives run so much smoother. This helps us to enjoy life more — feeling relaxed, rather than stressed. In control, rather than bounced around by outside forces. And with the space, energy and creativity to do what we want.

Just as your car can perform better, accelerate faster, drive more economically, and run more smoothly if you maintain it, so, too, can your life run more smoothly—if you take the time to find and maintain your happiness.

This leads us back to the question people ask. What does make us happy?

The answer is that it isn't things or experiences that make us happy. Happiness is a choice we either make or don't make. This sentence has many layers to it. Most people take it at the superficial level and can't understand why they don't feel happy.

It doesn't mean that you go about your business, putting yourself in all different kinds of situations where you feel bad, see only ugliness, and then choose to be happy. Of course that will not work.

At that level it is like being thrown in the sea with a lead weight and choosing to float. Words are far less important than what you really mean. If 95% of your thoughts and actions are directed to something other than happiness, but you say, "I choose happiness—"

You haven't really chosen happiness... you have just tried to fool yourself that you have.

For most people, happiness is an afterthought. They make the decisions that determine the course their life takes for a hundred other reasons—because it is expected of them, because they want to please other people, and because it's what they should do.

Then they end up out of their depth, flailing in the river of life. So they start to think, *I just want to be happy.* Somewhere they read that happiness is a choice. And so in their desperation for any life belt, in between making deals with God, they say, *Now I choose happiness.*

But it doesn't work, and never will work.

You can have any one thing you want from life... but only one thing at a time. Life is so interconnected and interwoven that one choice can block another.

For example, you, like most people, may want to be happy, successful, loved, and respected. These are your intentions. Tomorrow, a situation may arise that needs you to make a decision how to allocate your resources—either money, time, or whatever.

Now, using your resources to complete or begin a new project may bring you success, but work against your wish for love, as it takes you away from your loved ones.

Many, many times in a day, we are faced with these decisions between two or more intentions. And so what most of us do is to choose, say, success, then in the next choice switch to love, then to happiness, and so on.

This means that we start up one road, then go back and up another, then back and up another, over and over again. Despite all our efforts and travelling, we keep ending up where we were.

Those people who are most single-minded choose consistently. At every point, they choose the same thing. As a result, they go further and further down that road, leading to more success, love or happiness.

This, however, can lead to having one thing, but missing out on the rest. There is a way to have everything, but we'll discuss this later.

To choose happiness means going to sleep tonight having made the decision to be happy in the morning. Then whatever we decide or do, we do from happiness. We are happy so we...

This way, we never get into the situation where we start to flounder. We only ever get into trouble, when we make our decisions for any reason other than choosing happiness. Once we drift off the path, it is easy to get caught up in the whirlwind of life, and before we know it, we are so disorientated by life bouncing us around, we have forgotten who we are and what we really want.

Conventional wisdom tells us to make the best of what we have. If we have lemons, make lemonade. This is one of the main ways that we trap ourselves. Because we then believe that our life can only be as good as the raw materials we have and our ability to make something from these.

Instead, decide what you want and let that set the tone. Then gather the raw materials you need. When we look at what we currently have, we feel trapped and limited. When we start from a perspective of what we want, without limit, then we open up our imagination, creativity, and enthusiasm. This is where we gain the inspiration, energy, and ability to create whatever we want.

Tension restricts our perspective and traps us into situations with limited options. Being happy first broadens our perspective. We have more energy and creativity to see opportunities and act on them.

Feeling good, feeling happy and in love, is nature's guidance system. It is the way that we can know we are connected to the flow of life.

If we stay connected to that flow, our path is clear, and we have all the motivation, energy, and ability to do whatever we have to do.

When we feel anything other than happy and motivated, it is because we drifted off our path and started to listen to others.

You were never put here to buy a nice house in a quiet suburb, fit in with your neighbours, and make people feel good about the new dress they bought.

You are here as an expression of the evolutionary force of life to create new ways of expressing yourself. This is how you add value to the world. Not by becoming Clone No. 5890678.

So what does this mean? It means say what you think, do what makes you happy, and in Joseph Campbell's words, "follow your bliss". If you are happy and connected to the flow of life energy, your words or actions will not hurt anyone. To hurt another would create fear of retribution and so disturb your happiness. So many people say to this, "But I can't just worry about my happiness. I have responsibilities."

You cannot effectively fulfil your responsibilities without happiness. If I asked you to give me a million pounds, what would be your response? Probably something like, "It would be nice to have it, to give it." Even those who have millions would say something like "I'm not made of money" or "I earned mine through hard work and you should, too."

In other words, they believe that they only have so much money and so they cannot freely give away all they have. In the same way, unless you know that you can dip into a limitless source of happiness and create more happiness whenever you want... you can never freely give happiness.

A person, without happiness to smooth their words and actions, creates friction. Their actions may on the surface seem to help, but they are performed at a perceived cost to the person. This cost feels as if it is eroding the person, just as running a car without oil will damage its parts. And so they will sooner or later feel bitter or resentful and damaged by the wear and tear to their well-being in giving to another.

Throughout history, people have looked at limitless patience and acts of kindness by people like Jesus, Buddha, Lao Tsu, Mother Theresa, and so on. And they think, *This is a great example, I must live up to this.*

And they try to follow the actions. But they feel burnt out, eroded, and damaged. Then they beat themselves up and say, "I'm not as good as..."

They went off the path when they copied the actions. Effective, smooth action only comes after inspired thought. Inspired action can never follow frantic, panicked thought.

What they failed to understand, because they couldn't see it, was that these individuals were already happy. Then because happiness smoothed their actions and words, they didn't cause any friction or damage to others. And so they could do these acts of kindness and be infinitely patient without costing themselves anything. In the same way, events that may have looked hugely painful were not painful to these individuals.

It is not that they are unique or special, in the sense that you could not achieve what they did. It is just that they approached life from a radically different perspective that enabled them to seem superhuman.

We will talk later about the Economic Mindset. This is a perspective from which it seems that only actions have value... but this is only true on the more superficial layers of life. When operating from that perspective, though you may do something for another, you will in some way try to get rewarded, or you'll feel cheated.

Real happiness can never be bought or sold. Nor given or taken. It can only be chosen and enjoyed. You can never achieve enough to earn happiness. Nor can you manipulate circumstances enough to cause another to be happy.

More harm is done in this world by individuals, groups, and nations who act from the arrogance of believing they could possibly know the best way forward for another, than from any number of individuals who act for their own happiness.

When one person says this is the right way, another sees something different and she says, "No. This is the right way." Both are certain that they are right. And each is in their own little world.

So now there can only be one right way. And so begins the fight—either verbal, physical, or psychological. Neither side will rest until their way has been upheld. Instead of appreciating the best in the other, now both look for weakness and blame.

> Therefore if you bring your gift to the altar, and there remember that your brother has anything against you; Leave there your gift before the altar, and go your way; first be reconciled to your brother, and then come and offer your gift.

From The Sermon On The Mount

It is as if there is a balloon being blown up between them. The longer it goes on, the more distanced the pair become. The more distance, the more critical of each other they become. When they get far enough away from each other, there becomes nothing about the other that they like or see as worthwhile.

If you have an image of what is right for someone else, then that begins to strip away their free will. You may be doing it for the best of intentions, just wanting for them to be happy. But it is based on a belief that they need X to be happy. And so X is required for their salvation.

They don't.

They will find their own way to happiness if they are allowed and allow themselves. Whenever we hold an image that is best for another, we cannot help but try to shape them in that direction. And if they go in any way other than the direction we believe to be for the best, we think they are wrong.

Then we either tell them in one way or another that they are wrong, or the balloon comes between us and the distance grows between us. From this point on, you can only see the lost opportunities for the other.

We do not know enough to even work out what is best for ourselves, let alone another. There are so many variables and unseen opportunities to life that you can never calculate into your equations of what is best for one person. Not even the combined wisdom of ten people together would be able to plot the best way forward for an individual. All you can do is help them to access their own guidance and trust in themselves and the universe.

❋ *The Earth revolves anti-clockwise on an oscillating axis of 23.5°. There are 365 revolutions of the Earth during the time it takes the earth to complete its orbital journey around the Sun.*

THE WISE WOMAN'S STONE

A wise woman who was travelling in the mountains found a precious stone in a stream. The next day she met another traveller who was hungry, and the wise woman opened her bag to share her food.

The hungry traveller saw the precious stone and asked the woman to give it to him. She did so without hesitation. The traveller left, rejoicing in his good fortune. He knew the stone was worth enough to give him security for a lifetime.

But, a few days later, he came back to return the stone to the wise woman.

"I've been thinking," he said. "I know how valuable this stone is, but I give it back in the hope that you can give me something even

Source Unknown

more precious. Please give me what you have within you that enabled you to give me this stone.”

Sometimes it's not the wealth you have but what's inside you that others need.

4.
Overcome the Economic Mindset

We live our lives through what I call an Economic Mindset. By this, I don't mean that we equate everything to money. I mean that money is a reflection of the way we look at life.

We put values on actions, or inactions, and use this as the basis of our decisions.

Often I look around at peoples' decisions and their rationalisations, and it seems that many people are scared to give too much of themselves. The cultural equation for the ideal life seems to be the maximum you can get for the minimum you give. Yet study after study demonstrates that the more we do, the more we give, the more active we are... the better we feel.

You can see the Economic Mindset demonstrated when we feel we have to do or have something in order to be happy.

It is because of the Economic Mindset that we believe if a small amount of something is good, more must be better. And so we become addicts or over-indulgers.

According to figures from the U.S. Department of Agriculture, in the 50 years between 1950 and 2000 obesity rates have rocketed by 214 percent. We can clearly see the cause as in the 30 years from 1971 to 2000, U.S women have increased their daily calorie consumption by 22% and there is no sign of this reducing, despite all the talk of diets and healthier eating. Yet this mindset of overindulging is killing us. 280,000 Americans die every year from obesity.

We hate to exercise, yet we feel great afterwards.

We love to sit in front of the television, yet of any activity, it generates among the lowest levels of happiness.

The Economic Mindset is clearly seen in our relationships. The expectation is that if you do X, your partner will do Y. Then when your partner doesn't do Y — perhaps they never even knew it was expected — you feel cheated.

This feeling of resentment creates that same balloon we spoke about earlier between you and your partner. The longer it stays there, the more distance, bitterness, and unhappiness you will experience with your partner.

The Economic Mindset is particularly destructive in personal relationships. First of all, before the couple even gets together, there exists a fairytale image of romance. Boy meets girl and they fall in love. Sooner or later, the novelty of the relationship fades. Probably one or two issues have by now come between them.

Meanwhile, both individuals are still receiving the images through newspapers, magazines, people they see, TV programmes, and films of the ideal partner.

The media exists to sell products. There is no other reason. Sure, it informs and entertains, but it is a business. And it makes money from advertising. So all the information and entertainment exists for the purpose of distracting audiences to sell them things.

There are different types of advertising, but one of the most prevalent is aspirational. This is where the man wears a certain deodorant and suddenly women start throwing themselves at him. Or buys a certain car that gives him instant respect.

We take in all these images. Lots of people say to this, "Yes, but I don't pay attention to adverts." Studies show that even when people think that advertising doesn't influence them, it does. If it didn't, companies wouldn't spend the millions that they do.

We make sense of the world by putting together everything we see and hear and coming up with our own interpretation of how things work.

This is very important in relationships.

Why?

Because in our head, we hold two images of our partner: what they should be and what they are.

What they should be is based on all the examples we see of husbands and wives around us. As an example, here's how a woman (and, yes, of course men use a similar process) might use images as a benchmark for her relationship:

- the neighbour's husband bringing home flowers
- the friend being whisked away for a romantic weekend
- the charismatic lead in the film we saw last week
- a colleague's sense of humour and caring nature
- the physique of the man you see at your gym
- the wealth and power of someone else
- the dress sense of another
- the intelligence of another
- another who is nurturing

If you add up the total of the best of all these images, this is the total value of men to our fictional woman. Now this represents 100% of her ideal husband/partner.

Now she'll have some kind of idea of how much she believes she deserves. Now she'll rate herself in terms of her self-image.

Specifically she may use:

- how attractive she perceives herself to be
- her housework abilities and effort
- her personal qualities that she brings to the relationship
- her intelligence level, and so on

Each of us has our own unique images of potential partners and what we deserve. So when you are assessing a potential partner, you may unconsciously think, I'm worth about 60% of my ideal picture.

Then once you have begun the relationship, initially you show the best side of yourself. Not just that, but you will also tend to look at the more positive features of the other.

In time, the relationship settles down. Both put less effort in, because you get distracted by other things and also because you feel less need to. You are more comfortable with each other.

It's now that words, thoughts, and actions will start to pass unresolved between you. This creates that balloon. The longer between resolution, the more distanced you become.

It isn't really the things that your partner does that causes you to be upset with him or her. If you feel happy, what they do may be easily shrugged off by you. But if you have become ground down and irritated, you have far less tolerance and patience, and so what they do affects you far more. By working on being happy, you therefore are more accepting of your partner, and so you allow them to be as they are to a greater extent—without any loss or cost to you.

When you feel distanced, feelings of resentment and bitterness creep in. All of us are whole people. We have an enormous range of qualities—some you feel are positive, some negative. No one is completely positive or negative. We are each capable of experiencing all emotions and acting on each of these emotions.

If you feel bitter about someone, you will look at the aspects of that person that justify that bitterness. If you feel loving about someone, you will see those aspects of the person. However you feel about a person determines what you see in them.

This is why some people love someone, while others cannot see any redeeming features in the same individual.

The more distanced you become from your partner, the more aspects you will see that you dislike. As you do this, you re-rate your partner against your ideal rating. But now the score is much lower than before. And so you feel cheated.

The Economic Mindset demands that you get as much as you give. So you either:

- reduce the effort you put into the relationship
- feel bad
- have a relationship, with another person, to top up the gap between what you feel you give and what you get
- or, change your partner

Money is very important to the Economic Mindset because it is a way of putting value on people, their time, or their creations. We do not think through the Economic Mindset because of money; we have money because it is the physical manifestation of our Economic Mindset.

We grade peoples' worth by the value we ascribe to their creations. We sometimes determine our own self-worth by the value others place on us. Being paid more than our neighbour makes us feel that we are more highly valued, and so we relish status symbols. Being bought expensive presents and taken to expensive places makes us feel that we are treasured and so influences our self-valuation.

The problem with this perspective is that the value is inherently hollow. It is only a symbolic shell for real valuation. And so no matter how much surface value we gain, it will never be enough because it has nothing substantial that can nourish us on an emotional/spiritual level.

❋ *Aside from sunrise and sunset the sea does not reveal much about the Sun's behaviour. The most useful natural tool at sea is the wind, not only for finding direction but also for holding course, orientation and position.*

Local prevailing winds at sea cannot clearly be read, yet the sea can reveal the current and previous actions of the wind.

THE CARPENTER'S HOUSE

An elderly carpenter was ready to retire. He told his employer-contractor of his plans to leave the house-building business and live a more leisurely life with his wife, enjoying his extended family.

He would miss the paycheck, but he needed to retire. They could get by. The contractor was sorry to see his good worker go and asked if he could build just one more house as a personal favour. The carpenter said yes, but in time it was easy to see that his heart was not in his work. He resorted to shoddy workmanship and used inferior materials. It was an unfortunate way to end his career.

When the carpenter finished his work and the builder came to inspect the house, the contractor handed the front-door key to the carpenter. "This is your house," he said, "my gift to you."

What a shock!

Source Unknown

What a shame!

If he had only known he was building his own house, he would have done it all so differently. Now he had to live in the home he had built none too well.

So it is with us. We build our lives in a distracted way, reacting rather than acting, willing to put up less than the best. At important points we do not give the job our best effort. Then, with a shock, we look at the situation we have created and find that we are now living in the house we have built. If we had realised that earlier, we would have done it differently.

Think of yourself as the carpenter. Think about your house. Each day you hammer a nail, place a board, or erect a wall. Build wisely. It is the only life you will ever build. Even if you live it for only one day more, that day deserves to be lived graciously and with dignity. The plaque on the wall says, "Life is a do-it-yourself project."

Your life tomorrow will be the result of your attitudes and the choices you make today.

47

5.

Realise the Difference
Between a Hedonic High
and Authentic Happiness

The Economic Mindset causes us to look at the transactional and more superficial layers of life. Therefore, when we look at happiness, we have oversimplified its causes.

In life, every event, thought, word, and occurrence has many levels from the root to the fruit. Happiness is no different. At its root, happiness is purely the uninhibited and undistorted experience of life. At the physical level, happiness is simply a bio-chemical mix.

Just as we can turn pain into numbness with anaesthetics, we can create the sensation of happiness by changing the chemistry of our brain. Or we can think happy thoughts, which causes our brain to produce the same chemistry.

So the sensation of happiness can be observed and described in terms of neuro-chemistry.

Or the neuro-chemistry can be seen as a consequence of happiness.

Even though we may not have understood the precise blend of hormones and chemicals, we have noticed that certain occurrences have caused us to feel happier.

These occurrences are enhancers of—rather than the cause of—long-term happiness. Though, because of our Economic Mindset, and our limited understanding, we focused on the surface layer of circumstances, rather than the more stable underlying layer of attitudes and perceptions that created the situations we were in. So we mistakenly decided that the sensation of being happy is happiness.

Generation after generation has operated on the misunderstanding that if we created more sensations of happiness, we would be happier.

It is a mistake to base happiness on mood enhancers, whether that be favourable circumstances or chemical help, because by their nature, the high must be followed by a low.

True happiness is the uninhibited enjoyment of life, the true expression of your unique blueprint—not a momentary, emotional reaction.

This misunderstanding has created two interpretations of happiness.

These distinctions, first spoken of by the ancient Greeks such as Aristotle, are Hedonic and Eudaimonic happiness. Hedonic happiness is all about pleasure. Because our society operates on an Economic Mindset, it loves pleasure.

Pleasure gives us a chemical high—the physical and emotional sensation of happiness. It is easy to produce; and unfortunately, a necessary downside is that after the high comes the low. Pleasure is unsustainable, as it is based on a neurochemical reaction, which must then stabilise. This creates an addictive cycle and a need for continual excitement.

If you look around our society, there is a continual need for external sources of excitement.

What can I buy?
Where can I go?
What's the latest gossip?
What's the latest television programme/song/fashion?
I'm bored, what will excite me?

Drug addicts or alcoholics are treated as sick because of the outcomes of their addiction, yet look around and you will see:

- workaholics
- shopping addicts
- celebrity-trivia addicts
- exercise addicts
- sex addicts
- coffee addicts
- people addicted to the buzz of new relationships
- and on and on

Take someone who deals with her stress by "retail therapy". It doesn't matter what she buys; she has a wardrobe full of clothes that she hardly ever wears. When the pressure of work hits her, when she rows with her partner, the best way she knows of picking herself up is through retail therapy.

Because this addiction is not obviously harmful, nobody notices the damage it is doing. If she was shooting up heroin or drinking daily, her friends wouldn't go get her a fix or a bottle. Yet because it seems harmless, her friends will tell her, "You've had a hard time, you deserve a treat."

An addiction is an addiction, whether it is drugs, work, drink, or a television programme. The only difference is in intensity. The more intense the addiction, the more it affects the addict, the quicker the person cottons on. A junkie learns quickly that he must overcome the drugs or they will overcome him. The television addict spends her life in front of the television, then on her deathbed regrets the opportunities she has missed. Everyone knows drugs and alcohol can damage your body; yet we do not recognise the damage less toxic addictions do to us.

Physically, they cause the same up and down chemical effect. This leaves waste chemicals and uses up nutrients, likely to create deficiencies and imbalances. The difference between an intense addiction and an extremely mild one is that the drug addict can go through the same cycle in a couple of years, where the mild, socially acceptable addict may never even recognise it.

Mild addictions trap us in the myth of hedonic happiness. This prevents us from finding and knowing who we really are. They distract us from the emptiness inside. And so we may never overcome the emptiness of not knowing who we are.

As a direct result, we cannot truly connect with others, so our relationships suffer. The shopping addict has to keep her financial predicament a secret from her partner. This creates a balloon and starts to build a distance between them. And so problems spiral into crises.

There are hundreds of things people are addicted to that are admired because they support society. Yet the underlying dynamic is the same as the drug addict. The workaholic is held up as a model to "slackers" who want a life outside work, yet his children at home pine for a dad who cares about them.

We love pleasure because it supports our illusion of the Economic Mindset. It makes us rich, provides short term highs and most importantly, distracts us from our problems. But it is a trap — a trap that distracts us from living a truly blissful life: a journey that has us truly engaged with the mystery of life.

Read on to find out why the truth will set you free.

☀ *The rotation of the Earth —*
along with the high temperatures
generated by the Sun — are
together responsible for the
distribution of heat from the
Earth's equator to the poles...
wind, which in turn affects the
formation of the waves and
swells across the oceans.

PERSPECTIVES

One day a rich father took his young son on a trip to the country with the firm purpose to show him how poor people can be. They spent a day and a night in the farm of a very poor family. When they got back from their trip, the father asked his son, "How was the trip?"

"Very good, Dad!"

"Did you see how poor people can be?" the father asked.

"Yeah!"

"And what did you learn?"

The son answered, "I saw that we have a dog at home, and they have four. We have a pool that reaches to the middle of the garden, they have a creek that has no end. We have imported lamps in the garden, they have the stars. Our patio reaches to the front yard, they have a whole horizon."

Source Unknown

When the little boy was finished, his father was speechless.

His son added, "Thanks, Dad, for showing me how poor we are!"

Isn't it true that it all depends on the way you look at things? If you have love, friends, family, health, good humour, and a positive attitude toward life, you've got everything!

You can't buy any of these things. You can have all the material possessions imaginable, provisions for the future, etc., but if you are poor of spirit, you have nothing!

THE TRUTH SHALL SET YOU FREE.

6.

See the Deeper Meaning Behind
the Superficiality of Everyday Life

So what is it that traps us in the first place? To set the scene to explain this, first we need to understand how the reality we experience is created.

All of life is created from an energy force. This provides the source, the power, and the building blocks for everything that we see around us. This force then flows through our beliefs. It works like a kaleidoscope. What we see as we look out on our life is the life force shaped by our beliefs.

If what we see doesn't look or feel good, it is because of our beliefs. Change the beliefs and we change what we see and feel.

Life Force → Beliefs → Experience

The things we see around us are just symbols of our feelings. They relate to a feeling. Our experience of life is really just a demonstration of what we believe. Wherever there is something you don't enjoy, analyse your beliefs. Change them until you find something that works better for you.

There is no other higher purpose. Life just wants to expand itself. It can only do that as you increase the amount that you allow to flow through you.

Equally, as a part of life we want to grow. Through the Economic Mindset it seems that we are ambitious for material things, status and experiences. At the deeper levels, though, what we really want is evolution and the freedom to be ourselves. And so through the filter of our beliefs, we experience the desire for new clothes, things, and events.

Our drive comes through us in many ways: through ambition, our craving for sex, status, emotional connection, to create, and so on, the urge of life comes into the world, shaped through our unique perspective and beliefs.

We are driven to experience the flowing of life through us and into the world. We do this by creating something new.

This doesn't mean we are all here to invent new things. It means we are here to express our message. For example, our message may be a new way of teaching children or it may be standing up and highlighting the plight of the starving. It doesn't matter who you are; in some way, big or small, you are here to make a difference.

In order to achieve these deeper aims, we are guided through our feelings to the situations that enable us to tweak or change our beliefs. Each change of belief either reduces or expands the amount of life we allow into us.

Each choice either: opens us up to life, and so increases our health and happiness; or closes us to life, and so reduces our health and happiness.

If we only look on the surface levels, we only see the objects that we want. They range from a new partner to a new car or a new dress, or any other thing that you desire.

They in themselves are not the goal; they are but the means of moving you towards the goal. There is really no division between spiritual and physical pursuits. What is generally viewed as spiritual is the force underlying the desire for the physical. One level is the level of thought and ideas. The other is a physical expression of that idea. But you may, if you wish to view it that way, separate life into that which is spiritual and that which is physical. This is just an example of the way our beliefs determine what we see.

I know many people will misunderstand what I have just written, so here is an example. Say you want a new coat.

Why do you want a new coat?

Because your old one is out of date or becoming worn.

So what do you really want?

To look presentable or even attractive.

Why do you want to look attractive or presentable?

So that people won't think badly of you.

Why don't you want people to think badly of you?

Because they might not want to talk to you or get to know you.

So the symbol of a new coat is really about the idea of getting along with people and expanding your experiences through social interaction. The goal is the same as the more "spiritual" goal of living harmoniously with others, but it is disguised in a physical symbol.

Because we generally look on the surface layer with the Economic Mindset, we easily become fixated on the thing we want—the symbols. Sometimes we cannot get that thing. And so we feel frustrated and angry as we bang our heads against the wall endlessly to get it.

Yet if we looked from a broader perspective, we would see a fly who keeps bashing up against a closed window, despite there being an open window just a few feet away.

The important thing is to remember that the thing is not essential, it is just the symbol for the desired feeling. We can find another way of reaching the same feelings and so change our beliefs.

However, through the Economic Mindset, we lose sight of the real meaning of our desires. We become fixated on getting the object of our desire.

As we keep focusing on this thing—and yet can't achieve it—the effect is like a car stuck in a muddy field. So the harder we try, the more stuck we get. Eventually we have dug ourselves into a rut. If we keep spinning our wheels, we reach a point where we become so depressed that we can no longer see any other option. Now we're trapped—and powerless—just through our own thought process.

Therefore, it is helpful to recognise that any time you want something, it isn't really the thing you want... it is just moving you towards the experience the deeper part of you craves.

✳ *The size of waves are influenced by the strength of the wind, the amount of time it has been traveling and the fetch (distance travelled across open waters). Waves move forward carrying new energy with them. Ripples, waves and swells are evidence of the wind giving the water energy.*

FIND SOMETHING BEAUTIFUL

I had a very special teacher in high school many years ago whose husband died suddenly of a heart attack.

About a week after his death, she shared some of her insights with a classroom of students. The class was nearly over, and as the late afternoon sunlight came streaming in through the classroom windows, she moved a few things aside on the edge of her desk and sat down there.

With a gentle look of reflection on her face, she paused and said, "Before class is over, I would like to share with all of you a thought that is unrelated to class, but which I feel is very important."

"Each of us is put here on earth to learn, share, love, appreciate, and give of ourselves. None of us knows when this fantastic experience will end. It can be taken away at any moment.

Source Unknown

Perhaps this is God's way of telling us that we must make the most out of every single day."

Her eyes beginning to water, she went on, "So I would like you all to make me a promise. From now on, on your way to school, or on your way home, find something beautiful to notice. It doesn't have to be something you see; it could be a scent—perhaps of freshly baked bread wafting out of someone's house; or it could be the sound of the breeze slightly rustling the leaves in the trees, or the way the morning light catches one autumn leaf as it falls gently to the ground."

"Please look for these things, and cherish them. For, although it may sound trite to some, these things are the "stuff" of life. The little things we are put here on earth to enjoy. The things we often take for granted. We must make it important to notice them, for at any time... it can all be taken away."

The class was completely quiet. We all picked up our books and filed out of the room silently. That afternoon, I noticed more things on my way home from school than I had that whole semester.

Every once in a while, I think of that teacher and remember what an impression she made on all of us, and I try to appreciate all of those things that sometimes we all overlook.

Take notice of something special you see on your lunch hour today. Go barefoot. Or walk on the beach at sunset. Stop off on the way home tonight to get a double-dip ice cream cone. For as we get older, it is not the things we did that we often regret, but the things we didn't do.

7.
Use the Power of Attention Consciously

Information is power.
Wrong.
Knowledge is power.
Wrong.

At the surface level, where we place most of our attention, power seems to be about having things and controlling people and resources. So power appears to come from status and from possessions. Status implies that you can have influence over others, if not control.

Yet this is not authentic power. This is only symbolic power. It may impress those who mistake the symbols for the real thing, but ultimately it is impotent.

There are more variables and unknown quantities to life than anyone could list, let alone control. It doesn't matter how powerful you seem to be. In truth, you can never control even one other person. You may be able to coerce them into behaving in the way you wish for a period of time, but you will never force them to comply with you in mind, body, and spirit.

We only have to look at some of the most powerful people in history to see that however much power they held, they were still undone in numerous ways.

- Alexander the Great at the time was the most powerful man in history, yet he was dead by 33.
- Julius Caesar, all-conquering hero of Rome, was yet betrayed and killed by a supposed friend.
- Napoleon Bonaparte, one of the greatest Military Generals and the most powerful Emperor of his day, died stripped of power and exiled in St Helena. Reflecting in his later days he said this...

I know men and I tell you that Jesus Christ is no mere man. Between Him and every other person in the world there is no possible term of comparison. Alexander, Caesar, Charlemagne, and I have founded empires. But on what did we rest the creation of our genius? Upon force. Jesus Christ founded His empire upon love; and at this hour millions of men would die for Him.

Napoleon

The source of all power comes not from us, but through us, from the source of all life. This power is unlimited. Our beliefs determine how much of this power flows through us. Where the power goes is determines by what we focus our attention on.

So it is not knowledge, or information, that is power, but attention. Where we place our attention determines the knowledge and what information we gather. The extent to which we allow the power of life to flow through us determines how awake and alert we are.

The more awake and alert that we are, the more information around us we will notice and take in. The more conscious we are, the truer understanding of life we will have.

The truer the picture of life that we have and operate from, the more effective and powerful will be our understanding and philosophy of life.

Most people are completely unaware of the source of their power. And so they place their attention everywhere. This is like a hose where the water just splutters out weakly. Each splutter does not contain enough force to bring anything to life. Therefore, nothing much gets created.

In contrast, those who recognise the power and the value of focused attention have the power of a jet-like hose. They have the determination and the effectiveness to cut through problems like a laser. By directing all their attention into the same area, they provide enough energy to bring their dreams to life.

Whatever you are pointing your attention at, you are breathing life into. If your attention is focused on the shortcomings of others, you will notice these more. Remember every person is capable of a wide range of behaviours. Whichever levels and aspects of personality that you choose to see in that person, you will breathe life into — and so you will see more and more of in the future.

Have you ever looked at a friend's partner and thought, *What does he/she see in him or her?*

Well, what is happening is that your friend is focusing their attention on the positive aspects of the person — at least, they probably were in the beginning of the relationship. You are observing the negative. Therefore, you may both see entirely different sides to the same person. Perhaps in time if everyone says to your friend, "But look at this and this," they will start to put their attention in the same place as you. This, of course, breathes more life into those aspects, and you become proved right.

If you focus on what is wrong, more problems will crop up in your life. If you focus on your shortfalls, you breathe more life into them.

On the other hand, if you pay more attention to the good things that happen, you breathe more life into those. And more of the good stuff will show up in your experiences. If you pay attention to your strengths, you bring them to life and access those parts of yourself, and so become stronger, more capable, and more effective.

Life is infinitely flexible. You create your experience by your choices. Your most important choice is where to focus your attention.

✳ *The apparent colour of the sea is partially influenced by the reflection of the sky, as well as the organisms in the sea. Different levels of salt impact micro-organic life such as plankton. Gradual changes can be visible in the meeting of fresh water and brackish water. The levels of salt determine how blue or green the sea is: blue is salty, where as green indicates low salt levels.*

EVERYBODY KNOWS

EVERYBODY KNOWS:

You can't be all things to all people.
You can't do all things at once.
You can't do all things equally well.
You can't do all things better than everyone else.
Your humanity is showing just like everyone else's.

SO:

You have to find out who you are, and be that.
You have to decide what comes first, and do that.
You have to discover your strengths, and use them.
You have to learn not to compete with others.
Because no one else is in the contest of being you.

Source Unknown

THEN:

You will have learned to accept your own uniqueness.
You will have learned to set priorities and make decisions.
You will have learned to live with your limitations.
You will have learned to give yourself the respect that is due.
And you'll be a most vital mortal.

DARE TO BELIEVE:

That you are a wonderful, unique person.
That you are a once-in-all-history event.
That it's more than a right, it's your duty, to be who you are.
That life is not a problem to solve, but a gift to cherish.
And you'll be able to stay one up on what used to get you down.

8.

Invest Your Time Where It Will Reap the Greatest Reward

If our attention is the way that we can direct our power, time is the way our attention is organised. It enables us to see cause and effect. Yet in reality, time is only an illusion — an illusion we believe while our attention is directed towards the more superficial layers of life. So you can achieve your intentions far more quickly by moving into deeper layers and collapsing time.

Time, as we understand it, is a recent invention. It only really became particularly important to us at the beginning of the Industrial Revolution, once we started to organise ourselves into work groups. Running factories meant that people needed to turn up and get started at the same time. Ever since then, our lives have been organised around the dictates of the clock.

We see more evidence for this in the varying attitudes different cultures have to time. In most of the Western world, punctuality is very important. Other cultures may take a more flexible attitude to appointments.

Time, in reality, doesn't exist. It is only an interpretation of our experience. If you take Einstein's Law of Relativity to its logical conclusion, without any mass... time is no longer experienced. And therefore, all time becomes equally accessible.

We use time as a marker. It will take two years to do X. There is no reason that a set time is needed. The assumption is that in two years, you will have experienced certain occurrences. So if you could have had all these experiences within 6 months, you don't need to wait two years.

Here's the process to get whatever you want in life.

1. Focus only on what you want.
2. Identify what is between you and it.
3. Identify what is supporting that obstacle.
4. Take away the obstacle's supporting structures, until it collapses.
5. Repeat this until there is nothing between you and the thing you want.
6. Then it's yours.

This may seem obvious, but really obstacles exist only in your head. They are caused by you becoming stuck in one layer of life.

When you can move smoothly and freely in your thoughts, from the broad overview to the specific details, you can create whatever you choose.

Often people want to increase the length of their life. What they really want is to experience more. By increasing the velocity of their experiences, they can have the same experiences... and experience 140 or 210 years' worth of life in just 70 years.

This is how you can get more from life. It doesn't necessarily mean doing more. Often it is by slowing that we experience and savour more. Less is often more. Less distraction and clutter leads to more focused attention.

Everyone has the same time. It is the use of your time that determines the quality of your life. The key is to spend your time on those things that bring you passion and excitement, rather than those that dull and bore you.

Sometimes people talk in financial terms of the difference between residual or passive income streams and earned or active. Basically, if you work at a job or you sell your services, you get paid for the hours you work. This is active or earned income. If you create a product that once it's created, you can sell without spending any more time on, that's residual or passive income.

Put simply, it's the difference between being paid for your time by the hour or for the result of your work.

This concept also applies to us as individuals in how we spend our time and attention. Everyone has to grow or they'll get swamped and buried by life growing over them. Throughout your life you will have heartache, frustrations, and disappointments. There are two ways people approach these. You can identify with this because you are probably reading this book for one of two basic reasons:

Reason 1

Perhaps there is something in your life causing pain for you and you are looking for a way to heal it. Most people do this and once the pain has gone, they wait for another pain before they do anything else. This is active or earned growth. This way, you'll have more problems and you won't build up a great deal of momentum.

Reason 2

Or perhaps you worked out that by continually growing, you could prevent many problems from even showing up in your life. This can create a snowball effect so that you grow at a compounded rate. You still have to work at it... but the return on your time invested is much greater than if you only worked when life prodded you into it. Because when you deal with problems when they are still small, it's far easier to resolve them quicker than when they have grown into roaring great fires.

> Do the difficult things while they are easy and do the great things while they are small. A journey of a thousand miles must begin with a single step.

Lao Tzu

You can move from Reason 1 to Reason 2 by focusing on the following question. This will have the effect of putting you in control of your life—meaning that you won't get bounced around by life and will thus eliminate much stress, frustration, and misery, while creating joy, passion, and excitement.

If you were to rank your life experiences on a scale of 1–10, some of your life experience would be 1 and others 10. Why would you settle for less than 10?

If you focused your attention on this question sufficiently, it would stimulate you to wake up every morning, determined to make that day's experiences a 10. As your focus zoomed in on more rewarding life experiences, you'd get more of those.

We'll close this chapter with a way I have explained this concept that has worked powerfully for many people.

Imagine that you stand on the cliff overlooking the sea. Behind you is a bleak and ugly view. Before you is a beautiful sea view. And so you turn to look at the sea.

Now as you look this way, you see a gorgeous beach scene or the beauty of the sea. The sea has a greater pull for you and so your attention, like a camera's zoom, focuses there.

Where once you saw the overview, now you see it has many individual waves. Looking into the clear water, you can see fish. The sight of the fish draws your focus in.

Now you hone in one fish and see the marvel of its design. This creates a feeling of awe and inspiration.

This is how focus works in your life. You see more detail in whatever you focus on. Each separate detail will create different feelings in you. Life has everything—the full 360 degrees of experience. Good and bad. Pain and pleasure. And you are free to focus on whatever you choose. Whatever you choose will determine your experience of life.

☀ *Iolite is a precious stone, whose name derives from the Greek word 'ios' meaning violet. Viking mariners used thin pieces of iolite as the world's first polarising filter, as a navigation tool.*

The property that makes iolite so valuable is its extreme pleochroism. Iolite has different colours in different directions in the crystal. By looking through the crystal Vikings could see the direction of the Sun.

THE PENNY

Several years ago, a friend of mine and her husband were invited to spend the weekend at the husband's employer's home. My friend, Arlene, was nervous about the weekend. The boss was very wealthy, with a fine home on the waterway and cars costing more than her house.

The first day and evening went well, and Arlene was delighted to have this rare glimpse into how the very wealthy live. The husband's employer was quite generous as a host and took them to the finest restaurants. Arlene knew she would never have the opportunity to indulge in this kind of extravagance again, so was enjoying herself immensely.

As the three of them were about to enter an exclusive restaurant that evening, the boss was walking slightly ahead of Arlene and her husband. He stopped suddenly, looking down on the pavement for

Source Unknown

a long, silent moment. Arlene wondered if she was supposed to pass him. There was nothing on the ground except a single darkened penny that someone had dropped and a few cigarette butts.

Still silent, the man reached down and picked up the penny. He held it up and smiled, then put it in his pocket as if he had found a great treasure. How absurd!

What need did this man have for a single penny?

Why would he even take the time to stop and pick it up?

Throughout dinner, the entire scene nagged at her. Finally, she could stand it no longer. She causally mentioned that her daughter once had a coin collection, and asked if the penny he had found had been of some value.

A smile crept across the man's face as he reached into his pocket for the penny and held it out for her to see. She had seen many pennies before! What was the point of this?

"Look at it," he said. "Read what it says."

She read the words. "United States of America."

"No, not that; read further."

"One cent?"

"No, keep reading."

"In God we Trust?"

"Yes!"

"And?"

"And if I trust in God, the name of God is holy, even on a coin. Whenever I find a coin, I see that inscription. It is written on every single United States coin, but we never seem to notice it! God drops a message right in front of me telling me to trust Him? Who am I to pass it by?"

When I see a coin, I pray, and I stop to see if my trust IS in God at that moment. I pick the coin up as a response to God, that I do trust in Him. For a short time, at least, I cherish it as if it were gold. I think it is God's way of starting a conversation with me. Lucky for me, God is patient and pennies are plentiful!

When I was out shopping today, I found a penny on the side walk. I stopped and picked it up, and realised that I had been worrying and fretting in my mind about things I cannot change.

I read the words, "In God We Trust," and had to laugh. Yes, God, I get the message. It seems that I have been finding an inordinate number of pennies in the last few months, but then, pennies are plentiful! And God is patient.

9.

Manage Your Energy Wisely

You know how sometimes you'll see a cartoon character riddled with bullet holes, and for emphasis they take a drink and leak water everywhere? That is how most people live their lives. Their attention is spread over so many distractions that they have lost the ability to direct it and so create power and choice in their experience.

They go seeking more money. More self-esteem, more happiness, more excitement, more energy, and more enthusiasm. Yet it doesn't matter how much more they get, because as soon as they get it, they promiscuously spill it all over the place.

As a result, people go through life feeling empty and lacking. And whatever they do to get more... costs more to get. So no matter what they do, they never get ahead.

We can see this demonstrated in most people's relationship to money. However much they earn, they spend almost all their income, and often more. If they start earning more, their cost of living goes up with their income. So no matter how much they earn, they never retain anything. Often it just means that they have bigger debts.

Because this underlying philosophy drives other areas, we see the same thing happening in other aspects of life.

They want more attention, yet no matter how much more they get, it's never enough; they need more because whatever they get in, they leak it straight out again.

The leaks come from all the things we give our energy, attention, and thought to outside of us:

- Conflicts
- The newspaper article that gets us steamed up
- TV shows
- Gossip
- Doing things or promising to do things when every cell in our body shouts no, but we are too afraid to say no

In short, everything we ever do is caused by being too inhibited to stand up and say, "This is me. This is who I am. This is how I feel, and this is what I am going to do."

We can fix these leaks by first noticing them.

We can then identify why we allow our energy to just trickle out of us. This understanding, once it is brought into the open, takes away most of its sting.

We become controlled (by people or events) when we feel as if we have no choice. When we reach the understanding that everything in our life is created by us, or in conjunction with us, we can no longer act powerless. Then we once again have to make the decision of whether we will change or not.

Often even when people understand why they do what they do — which is mostly irrational — they still continue to do it. Even knowing that it is without good reason. This is because emotionally they cling onto the deeper beliefs that uphold this behaviour.

In the next chapter, I'll show you the most powerful shift in thinking you can ever make. This is the mindset that creates billionaires, world-famous artists, social reformers, inventors, and others who change the course of history.

※ *Clouds are produced as landmass pushes moist air higher, causing condensation and the formation of clouds. It is not only the existence, but also the size and shape of the clouds, that indicate the where-abouts of the land.*

THE BUTTERFLY

A man found a cocoon of a butterfly. One day a small opening appeared. He sat and watched the butterfly for several hours as it struggled to force its body through that little hole. Then it seemed to stop making any progress. It appeared as if it had gotten as far as it could, and it could go no further.

So the man decided to help the butterfly. He took a pair of scissors and snipped off the remaining bit of the cocoon.

The butterfly then emerged easily. But it had a swollen body and small, shrivelled wings.

The man continued to watch the butterfly because he expected that, at any moment, the wings would enlarge and expand to be able to support the body, which would contract in time.

Source Unknown

Neither happened!

In fact, the butterfly spent the rest of its life crawling around with a swollen body and shrivelled wings. It never was able to fly.

What the man, in his kindness and haste, did not understand was that the restricting cocoon and the struggle required for the butterfly to get through the tiny opening were God's way of forcing fluid from the body of the butterfly into its wings so that it would be ready for flight once it achieved its freedom from the cocoon.

IO.

Connect to Your Own Source

Just as a lamp needs electricity, humans need physical, emotional, and spiritual energy. It is this need to find sources of energy that drives all of our activities. Mostly, we end up opportunistically chasing whatever seems to have the best potential payoff. As a result, we focus our attention haphazardly. This is causes us to diffuse our power.

Our energy and enthusiasm levels depend on our biochemistry. Excitement is created by having adrenaline coursing through your veins. Your biochemistry can be affected by drugs or environment, but most persistently, it is determined by your thoughts.

To apply this concept, let's look at what the average person goes through in a day.

We wake up in the dark to an alarm clock. This means, biochemically speaking, the body is still asleep. Naturally, we are designed to wake up when sunlight excites the pituitary glands to release hormones. Our body's biochemistry then changes from the state of sleeping to the state of being awake and alert.

Since we wake up drowsy, we drink coffee to kick-start our system. This causes a high and then a low—borrowing energy now to repay later with interest.

Then we start our first of many interactions with those around us. We look at their mood, which determines how we act. Their mood is important to us, because it determines the nature of the energy we exchange with that person.

Mostly, we'll adapt our behaviour to try to change the mood of the other person—to get the positive energy we're seeking to exchange with them. Draining energy long term to get energy short term. Again, borrowing now to repay later.

Then we go into a job that may demand that we compromise our beliefs and principles. We do this because we believe we need the wage to survive. Money equals a form of energy, so we get energy, but at the high cost of our own emotional energy.

The various conflicts and compromises necessary for many people working together in a typical corporate culture create more of an energy drain. But often, we will gladly give up our energy, and change the way that we act, if we think it will gain us energy through praise, attention, recognition, etc.

Then we go home and drain our energy worrying about friends and family. We sit in front of the TV, waiting for it to stimulate us and so give us energy. Yet it is draining us of energy by distracting us from our own limitless reservoir.

But someone who plugs into their own source of energy doesn't have to expend energy to get energy from other people. They don't have to act out, showing off or whatever else in order to feel good from other people. They focus on themselves, so the energy builds up in them. Because they have plugged the holes most people have, they have their own energy source whenever they need it.

If you are thinking dull thoughts, your body doesn't believe that you need energy or alertness; so it won't release the hormones and chemicals that make you feel alert and energetic.

If you look at young children, they have boundless energy. Why?

Because they allow themselves to get excited by their thoughts. They don't check every thought to be sure it is practical or realistic. They don't feel they have to have every single detail controlled and worked out. They just follow what excites them. So they never lack energy and motivation.

Gossip, TV, films, music, taking unnecessary or reckless risks, getting engrossed in tragic accidents, and so on, are all ways that we use the world to create excitement for ourselves. But every attempt to gain energy from outside of us involves giving up energy to gain some.

In the long run, we end up with no more energy than we started with. It's all leaked away in the search for more. It becomes an addiction, rather like gambling. You win. Then you spend more to win again, and you hit a losing streak. Besides which, the energy we have becomes less pure as it comes contaminated with its own baggage.

These sources of energy do not create anything or invest any of you in them. So rather than expanding and adding to life — you are merely maintaining what is. This relates to the idea of residual growth and earned growth that we spoke of in Chapter 8.

All of nature grows organically. Plants and trees grow through their own roots. Humans believe we have to contort ourselves to become worthy of getting everything we need.

People often don't like to, or find it difficult to think of themselves in these kinds of ways, so it may be easier to look at how businesses make the same mistake.

Every successful business has one thing in common. It does something, perhaps only one minor thing, differently than everyone else.

What makes the difference between a Bill Gates, a Warren Buffet, or an Anita Roddick from the millions of other wannabe entrepreneurs?

The answer is in the wannabe. Each of these successful entrepreneurs, like hundreds of other multi-millionaires, started out with a passion. It was following their passion in their own unique way that made them successful.

Meanwhile, all the wannabes are focusing their energies outside of them — analysing the tactics and strategies that made these millionaires. But the secret is not in specific strategies or techniques; these are the fruit of the tree, but they only work because they grow organically from the trunk.

When Japan suddenly became an almost overnight economic success, many businesses went over to study what they were doing. Soon there were lots of books hitting the headlines with the techniques claiming to be the secret to Japan's success. Hundreds of companies started to change their ways to use these techniques.

For some, these worked out, but very few came anywhere near achieving the same success as the Japanese firms. This is because the techniques that Japanese companies were using were their natural responses to their particular situation, given their historical and cultural background. They grew organically from the essence of the company, rather than being fitted together as a secret formula.

Taking these ideas into companies in the Western world is like pulling apples from an apple tree and trying to fix them on a pear tree. The attitudes and beliefs of the people in the company, the company's relationship with its workers and so on, are different due to centuries of cultural evolution. So it is always going to be very difficult, perhaps impossible, to transplant something from one organism to another—whether that organism is a person, plant, or company.

In every major community now, you'll see billboards, leaflets, or ads promising you £5,000 a week for five hours of work. The market for business opportunities is huge. This is entirely because very few people are their own source. If a person is sourcing her ideas and excitement from herself, she will be overflowing with potential opportunities to profit from her interests and activities.

None of it is about the money; it is about finding new ways of expressing yourself. Work becomes art. And along the way, you find the perfect way to receive compensation for your artistry.

What happens is that when people get disconnected from their own source, they look externally for ideas, money, and energy.

So you begin looking for the answer outside of yourself. This diffuses the focus and potential power of your attention and consequently makes you too weak to create what you want from your own source.

Yet each individual, however weak and powerless they may seem or behave, has an infinite amount of power. If you doubt that you contain the power to create the circumstances you choose in your life—despite all the individuals in various circumstances throughout history who have managed to do so —consider this fact:

If all the energy coursing through every atom in your body right this minute were released, it would be sufficient to blow up the entire planet.

What you can do with all that energy depends entirely on how effectively you direct your attention. Whatever you focus on will be brought to life.

What do you choose to bring to life?

☀ *The anticlockwise revolution of the Earth means that wherever we are on Earth the Sun always appears due East and disappears due West. The position of the Sun in relationship to the celestial equator changes over the year, setting on the horizon with a declination of 23.5°.*

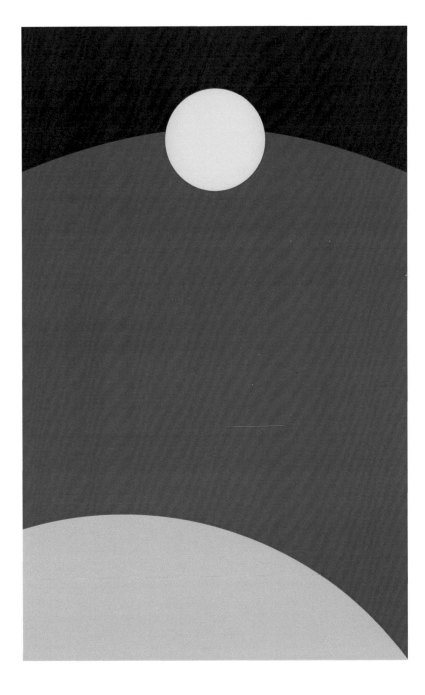

UNCONDITIONAL LOVE

A soldier was finally coming home after having fought in Vietnam. He called his parents from San Francisco.

"Mom and Dad, I'm coming home, but I've a favour to ask. I have a friend I'd like to bring home with me."

"Sure," they replied, "we'd love to meet him."

"There's something you should know" the son continued, "he was hurt pretty badly in the fighting. He stepped on a land mine and lost an arm and a leg. He has nowhere else to go, and I want him to come live with us."

"I'm sorry to hear that, son. Maybe we can help him find somewhere to live."

Source Unknown

"No, Mom and Dad, I want him to live with us."

"Son," said the father, "you don't know what you're asking. Someone with such a handicap would be a terrible burden on us. We have our own lives to live, and we can't let something like this interfere with our lives. I think you should just come home and forget about this guy. He'll find a way to live on his own."

At that point, the son hung up the phone. The parents heard nothing more from him. A few days later, however, they received a call from the San Francisco police. Their son had died after falling from a building, they were told.

The police believed it was suicide. The grief-stricken parents flew to San Francisco and were taken to the city morgue to identify the body of their son.

They recognised him, but to their horror, they also discovered something they didn't know: their son had only one arm and one leg.

The parents in this story are like many of us. We find it easy to love those who are good-looking or fun to have around, but we don't like people who inconvenience us or make us feel uncomfortable. We would rather stay away from people who aren't as healthy, beautiful, or smart as we are. Thankfully, there's someone who won't treat us that way. Someone who loves us with an unconditional love that welcomes us into the forever family, regardless of how messed up we are.

II.

Build a Solid Foundation
for Your Life

Do you remember the story of the three little pigs? You know, the one where the three pigs go off and build their own houses.

One is in a rush and quickly builds a house out of straw. The second builds a house from wood, and the third takes his time to build a solid home from bricks.

Then the big bad wolf blows down the first two pigs' houses because they never spent the time to get the foundations right.

But because the third one prepared his properly, he is safe from the wolf.

This relates to the way that we set up our lives.

Just as the first little pig built his house from straw, many people base their life around one thing, such as their work or a relationship. But the problem with this is that if something catastrophic happens to that thing, the individual's life will come crashing down. What do you do when your purpose for living has gone?

The second little pig bases her life on a number of pillars — such as family, work, hobbies, and so on. She might have a partner, children, work, hobbies, friends, and so on.

The danger is that she is still being supported or propped up by things external to her.

I have come across people who have led what most would call a balanced and healthy life. They had many interests and a wide "support network". Unfortunately, sometimes a sequence of events — or even, rarely, a single event — has taken away all the pillars that were holding up their life. This causes these individuals to feel somewhere from depressed to suicidal.

And most people would say that they are entitled to feel that way.

The question is: do you want the quality of your life determined by what happens to you? Or do you want to become the author of your own life?

Life always will throw out situations and obstacles to block what you think you want. You can either, as most people do, become frustrated, bitter, angry, or disillusioned — or, from this minute forward... you can determine to live a life of passion, excitement, and joy, regardless of what life throws at you.

This is what the third little pig chose. When there was no danger and no reason to put in any more than minimal effort, he still gave his best. As a result, he was prepared and immune to the threat of the big bad wolf.

Your choice is to put in as little effort as you need to now and hope that the gods look kindly on you — or to prepare yourself for what life is about to throw at you, so that when it comes it doesn't affect you. If you choose to prepare yourself, use the third little pig's strategy.

This is to create an overriding strategy or philosophy of life, one that drives every thought, word, and action in your life. Of course, life still contains the same people and passions, but they are enjoyed rather than needed.

Some people don't like the thought that they aren't needed or don't need others. If you need others, you are with them because you have to be. If you don't need them, you are free to go at any time and so are with them from choice, to enjoy them. Need creates pressure on both sides, whereas freedom relaxes both sides allows them to express their best selves and focus on the positive aspects of the other.

You may think that this could never happen to you, but it does to some people. What if all the people you loved were together travelling or at a party when there was a huge accident, leaving you the only one still alive?

What if that accident caused you permanent and serious health problems? These problems prevent you from doing your work and your hobbies. Think this is fanciful? I have spoken to people who have had this happen to them through one event and others who, through a course of events over a year, have had their lives devastated.

In life, you never know what is going to happen. I remember when the World Trade Centre buildings were brought crashing down. The most shocking thing to me was not the fact that these huge buildings could be destroyed. It was that people couldn't believe that they could be brought down.

Many things like that amaze me. I'm astounded that it is so rare for cars to mount the pavement. Or that traffic lights don't just suddenly go crazy, causing massive accidents. The point is that there are hundreds of things in our world that work even though they could at any moment stop working. So to me when the WTC was attacked, it wasn't a great surprise. But to many, it was unthinkable.

Why?

Because they used mental shortcuts that make them assume that tomorrow is going to be like today, with a different date. Most of the time, it is. Some research indicates that we have 60,000 thoughts a day. And 55–57,000 are the same ones as the previous day. This saves us mental energy, but it also covers up many flaws in our operating system.

As a result, we think because the WTC is so huge and impressive, it can never be destroyed. We think that because property prices have risen for the last five years, they will rise tomorrow. We think because our partner is fit and strong today, they will still be there in twenty years.

But that's not necessarily true. Life is an ever-renewing cycle.

Birth → Maturity → Death → Renewal

The problem is that most people never think about this. They live from moment-to-moment, day-to-day, without an overall strategy for life guiding their decisions and actions. This doesn't mean a plan guiding toward one grandiose life goal. It means fitting every moment into a deeper understanding of life. Without this, they often invest much of themselves in work, or relationships, in an attempt to achieve security or meaning. Then when things don't work out as they hoped, they feel cheated, resentful, and frustrated.

Perhaps they sacrifice pursuing their passion for the sake of their partner. Then five or ten years later, he or she dies or runs off with someone else.

Or maybe they sacrifice everything to climb the corporate ladder, but just as they touch the top rung, they get made redundant with no hope of a similar position. Then they find their family has moved on without them, and they have nothing left.

The devastation, resentment, and utter despair caused by these kinds of scenarios wrecks peoples' lives. It causes some to commit suicide. Since everything they believed and trusted in has been exposed as flawed, they do not know how to go on and trust again. It can cause a paralysis, as their operating system grinds to a halt. So they then have to rebuild it completely.

All because they trusted in things that had no solid basis. The last few centuries have given us many examples of how this type of thinking causes problems.

In the 1630s, there was a spectacular boom in the market for tulips. It sounds ridiculous now—as many of our fads will be to future generations—but the rich spent a lot of money on tulips. They became a status symbol, as they were rare and considered of great beauty.

Speculators noticed an opportunity to buy the rights to tulip bulbs, which would produce tulips to sell for vast profits.

They made out like bandits, and the news spread. Tulips became the hot tip, and more and more investors put their money in to them. The price rose and rose. Excitement grew about this sure thing, to the extent that people sold their house to buy a few tulip bulbs. Then one day, the price got too high, and tulips went out of fashion and became almost worthless. The unthinkable happened.

This has happened again and again. The South Sea Bubble, the 1920s crash, the 1980s, and so on. And the same thing happens to individuals with their relationships, their careers, and their personal lives—over and over again. All because of our flawed operating systems.

Your work, your health, and the people you care most about may not always be there. Never take anything in the world for granted.

Now is all there is. The past has gone, and who knows what the future will bring?

Sacrifice is never necessary. It's used when two wants are thought to be mutually exclusive. You can have both wants, but you need to be flexible and step your thinking to a higher level that allows both wants.

THE MAN BY THE WINDOW

Two men, both seriously ill, occupied the same hospital room. One man was allowed to sit up in his bed for an hour each afternoon to help drain the fluid from his lungs.

His bed was next to the room's only window. The other man had to spend all his time flat on his back.

The men talked for hours on end. They spoke of their wives and families, their homes, their jobs, their involvement in the military service, where they had travelled to. And every afternoon when the man in the bed by the window could sit up, he would pass the time by describing to his roommate all the things he could see outside the window.

The man in the other bed began to live for those one-hour periods where his world would be broadened and enlivened by all the activity and colour of the world outside.

Source Unknown

The window overlooked a park with a lovely lake. Ducks and swans played on the water, while children sailed their model boats. Young lovers walked arm in arm amidst flowers of every colour of the rainbow. Grand old trees graced the landscape, and a fine view of the city skyline could be seen in the distance.

As the man by the window described all of this in exquisite detail, the man on the other side of the room would close his eyes and imagine the picturesque scene. One warm afternoon, the man by the window described a parade passing by. Although the other man couldn't hear the band, he could see it in his mind's eye as the gentleman by the window portrayed it with descriptive words.

Days and weeks passed. One morning, the day nurse arrived to bring water for their baths only to find the lifeless body of the man by the window, who had died peacefully in his sleep. She was saddened and called the hospital attendants to take the body away.

As soon as it seemed appropriate, the other man asked if he could be moved next to the window. The nurse was happy to make the switch, and after making sure he was comfortable, she left him alone.

Slowly, painfully, he propped himself up on one elbow to take his first look at the world outside. Finally, he would have the joy of seeing it for himself. He strained to slowly turn to look out the window beside the bed. It faced a blank wall. The man asked the nurse what could have compelled his deceased roommate who had described such wonderful things outside this window. The nurse responded that the man was blind and could not even see the wall. She said that perhaps he just wanted to encourage you.

There is tremendous happiness in making others happy, despite our own situations. Shared grief is half the sorrow, but happiness when shared, is doubled.

I 2.

See Through Perceptual Illusions

Everything in life depends entirely on perception. The man in the story above was happy at the scene described to him, but it wasn't what actually happened that made him happy... it was what he thought was happening.

If you took five people at random and showed them the same picture, each would probably remember different things and have a different interpretation of what was happening. This is due to our perceptual filters.

I remember a man I once worked with in a temporary job while I was at college. He illustrates this concept so vividly.

Whatever happened, or was said, he could only see the bad in. He and I were in the same position. We'd both started working on a temporary basis in the summer. Christmas, the company's busy time, was coming up, but we were under no illusions that we weren't only there on a day-to-day basis for as long as they needed us.

John worked frantically. After a couple of weeks, the manager congratulated him on being the most productive worker the previous night. He also added that they were busy and there was a good chance of being kept on until Christmas. I interpreted this as encouragement. John shared his interpretation.

"He must think I'm a right ★★★★. He tells me I'm doing well, then in the next breath he's telling me I'm out the door at Christmas."

This was in July and he'd had no promise of work beyond the week. Yet John couldn't seem to allow himself to feel good about anything. Instead he focused on the negative... the subtle reminder that he was only there on a temporary basis.

He rapidly became known for his ability to see the worst in anything. People used to tell him things, just to see how he'd react. The only time John was pleased was when something bad happened to someone else. He was so afraid and had so little faith in himself that he needed others to fail to feel equal or superior to them.

One of the temporaries, who'd been there for two years compared to John's six months, was taken on permanently. He told John. John's reply was, "Well, that's me ★★★★★★★★ then." There was no congratulations, no good feeling. I saw him later, and he poured out his bitterness, feeling he should have gotten the job. John thought he worked harder, which was true.

However, the culture at this company was such that jobs generally went on the basis of how long you'd been there, unless you did something to upset someone. Rather than accept this and take it as encouragement that sooner or later he would be taken on, John saw it as a personal rejection. John had always been the hardest working, but then along came someone younger and faster who got on with the manager. He hated him. John believed that his face didn't fit. He thought he would be seen as too old to be given a job.

It became a game to feed John's fears. He took in everything negative because it fitted with what he believed. This worked him up into anger and bitterness about everything. After a while, we got fed up of winding John up and began avoiding him. Just talking to him was draining. He rowed with the managers and supervisors over petty things that only meant a lot to him. This isolated John.

As a result, he pushed himself down the list by antagonising the management. A quiet patch hit in February, and we were laid off for a couple of days. Then they only needed three of us for a few days. John, through his fear, had made himself disliked and was not picked among the three to come back. However, he was so frightened that perhaps he was the only one to be laid off that he turned up at work on his own time to check. When he saw other temporaries there, he flipped and rowed with the supervisor.

John created the very outcomes he feared by distorting situations to match his pessimistic beliefs.

Whatever your circumstances in life, they are created by you through your perception. Imagine that all the possibilities of life were spread across a 30cm ruler. Now, think of all the experiences humans have reported. Out of body experiences... mystic visions... psychic phenomena... seeing aliens... lifting a car to free a trapped child, and thousands more.

What we as an individual see and understand about life is equivalent to a 1mm groove. In any given situation, we have hundreds of options. Often, though, we become so stuck in our groove that we only see one or two options. So we do not think it is possible to experience all the types of opportunities listed above. And it isn't, while you are stuck in the groove you are currently in. But if you change the groove... you change the possibilities.

So if you do not like the circumstances in your life, you need to choose a different wavelength and tune into that. This will change your perception, and so you will have an entirely different experience of life. Your outward circumstances need not even change — though they probably will — and your experience of life will be completely different.

Our perceptual filters enable us to make sense of the world. Without them, we will be completely overwhelmed with information and unable to mentally function.

When we think of the world and our position in it, we imagine ourselves as if God has placed us in a world that wouldn't notice if we were here or not. But this is not really a true representation.

It sounds like a work of science fiction, but picture standing in nothingness and having 3 million separate pieces of information whizzing past you every minute. That is actually a truer picture of how our experience of life is created. However, it would be impossible to be able to relate to anything else thinking like this. And the key purpose of life is the ability to demonstrate your beliefs in relation to everything around you.

What we do is set up a kind of mental organisational system. We try to reduce all those separate pieces of information into just the ones that we need at that moment.

One of the key things we do is to take in less information about familiar environments and routines. You know how when you go into someone else's house, it often has a distinct odour, but you've become so used to your own home's scent that it doesn't register.

Or how someone else can notice your kids have grown, when you don't. This is all because this information is less important for you to perceive. Therefore your perceptual filters discard it. You only get the information that your organisational system believes is most important for you to know. Usually you do not notice the temperature, but if it is brought to your attention or it becomes uncomfortable, you'll start to pay attention to that information.

For this reason, we often keep doing stuff long past when it makes sense, just because it is a habit.

There is a story of a man who marries into an Italian-American family that illustrates how we do things just out of habit. Every year the whole family meets up for a Thanksgiving meal where they eat roast beef. At first, he goes to his girlfriend's house and watches, silently bemused, as her mother cuts the ends off the meat.

After marrying and setting up home, they host the Thanksgiving meal. Year after year, he watches his wife cut the ends off the meat. One day he can contain himself no longer.

He asks her why she always cuts the ends off the beef. She pauses for a moment, as if she has never considered the possibility of cooking it any other way, and then answers that it is how her mother always cooked it.

Intrigued, he asks her mother why she cooks beef that way. She is also surprised and says that is how her mother always cooked it. He turns to the grandmother and asks her why she cooks beef that way.

She says, "I don't any more, but when we first came over from the old country, we lived in a small cramped flat. When I cooked meat, my oven was very small and I had to cut it so that it would fit into the oven. Of course, I don't do that any longer."

How many areas of your life are you still doing things that make no sense?

When we first learn a new skill, whether it is learning to drive or to cook, we devote a lot of attention to it. We learn the reasons why we do something. These beliefs are the pillars that support the behaviour

As we become used to doing something, we just start to do it automatically. Our attention drifts somewhere else where the information is more relevant. Therefore, we often forget what our beliefs are. We can't walk around every minute knowing every belief; that would be like having every piece of software running on your computer at the same time. It would stop you from being able to do anything.

However, the problem is that many times, circumstances change, as in the roast beef story; and because we have forgotten the reasons why we are doing the behaviour we do, we do things that logically make no sense. This is all a side effect of the need to focus our attention.

❋ *The effect of the wind on snow is comparable to that between wind and sand. Cumulative effects are key to all wind forms, even if they are the result of only a few hours. These forms tend to be more reliable than using the current wind itself.*

THE WEIGHT OF THE GLASS

Once, a professor began his class by holding up a glass with some water in it. He held it up for all to see and asked the students, "How much do you think this glass weighs?"

"1 pound!" …"2 pounds!" …"3 pounds!" …the students answered.

"I really won't know unless I weigh it," said the professor, "but, my question is: what would happen if I held it up like this for a few minutes?"

"Nothing," the students said.

"OK, what would happen if I held it up like this for an hour?" the professor asked.

"Your arm would begin to ache," said one of the students.

Source Unknown

"You're right; now what would happen if I held it for a day?"

"Your arm could go numb, you might have severe muscle stress and paralysis and have to go to hospital for sure," ventured another student. All the students laughed.

"Very good. But during all this, did the weight of the glass change?" asked the professor.

"No," replied the students.

"Then what caused the arm ache—the muscle stress? Instead, what should I do?"

The students were puzzled. "Put the glass down," said one of the students.

"Exactly!" said the professor. "Life's problems are something like this. Hold them for a few minutes in your head; they seem OK. Hold them for a long time; they begin to ache. Hold them even longer; they begin to paralyse you. You will not be able to do anything."

It is important to think of the challenges in your life, but EVEN MORE IMPORTANT to "put them down" at the end of every day before you go to sleep. That way, you are not stressed; you wake up every day fresh, strong, and can handle any issue and any challenge that comes your way!

Remember friend—PUT THE GLASS DOWN TODAY!

13.
Appreciate the Impact and Power of the Human Operating System

Even with our perceptual filters blocking out most of the information that we receive, we still need some way of making sense of the rest of it.

So all the information gets processed into a mental framework. The mental framework is like a scaled-down model of the real thing. It misses some of the details, but broadly, it looks the same. A little like Google Maps provides a pretty good—but not exact or up-to-date—representation of a real area, so, too, does our Operating System represent life around us.

We start out having certain genetic tendencies. These influence the way that we react to situations. So each baby will interpret and react to the same stimulus in different ways, depending on their temperamental traits. So each is already starting to build up his or her own Operating System.

You've probably read that we only use 10% or less of the potential of our brain. Here's what that is based on:

All of us have billions of neurons at birth. The first time we process new motions, thoughts, and actions, these build a neural pathway by connecting neurons. The newborn baby responds to its interpretation of an event in the best way it knows how.

This creates a fresh path, like footprints in the snow. The next time the baby interprets an event needing the same response, he takes the easiest route, which is following the previous footsteps. Sometimes he will add a new step, or branch off slightly.

By the time he gets to be, say, six or seven, there are clear pathways.

By the age of seven, 70% of all the neural connections your brain ever will make are made. It's not that we can't make more connections. But most of us do the same things over and over again; we become stuck in our ruts. Therefore, we rarely do new activities and so we don't create many new connections.

Like walking across a field, it's easier to follow where others have walked before. The more you respond in the same way, the harder it is to do something differently. The pathway turns into a rut, and in time, to a ditch—until eventually it is almost impossible to see any alternative.

New actions that require unfamiliar responses, such as learning to drive, will create new pathways. But when you lift a drink to your lips, you use the same pathway you used to drink your bottle as a baby. When you throw something in anger, it is the same pathway you built throwing your toys from your pram.

Most movements and thoughts are refinements of pathways built in childhood. They all start out along the same path, but in time we give ourselves more options. The more options we have, the more effective we will be.

If you have a powerful emotional reason to do something differently, you will. For example, if you usually eat cake with a coffee, you probably automatically reach for it and eat it. But if you had a coffee after the doctor has just scared you out of eating cake, you'll catch yourself and stop.

Most of life is conducted on autopilot. We are only capable of doing so much, but the more we automate the mundane stuff, the more we can do. Therefore, we only pay attention to the things that are most important to us at this moment. The rest we delegate to our own personal assistant — our subconscious.

When we need to act, unless we have any reason to believe the situation needs a great deal of attention — such as being very dangerous — we take the quickest option. We forget all the reasons why we act as we do, and just respond as we normally do.

For this reason, most of our lives are conducted on automatic pilot. Therefore, our actions are controlled by our operating system. So the most important changes you can make to your life are those in your operating system. But by its nature, we are unaware of most of what is in our operating system.

Yet every decision you make determines the path you take through life. And almost all of these are decided through your operating system without your even being aware of making the decision.

Just a small shift in beliefs can create huge differences in your experience of life. Because the deeper and more buried the belief, the greater the trajectory of change. Changing one of your core fundamental beliefs will change many other beliefs along the way to your actions, and so into your experience.

Think of an aeroplane flying thousands of miles. Being just one degree out can lead to being hundreds of miles from the planned destination. Yet the nature of flying means that pilots spend most of their journey being off course. Their job is to continually adjust to get back on track and eventually where they want to be.

Humans, though, expect to learn the rules — to understand right and wrong — and then never deviate off track. To just mindlessly go through life, reach the destination, and everything will be fine. When we do drift off track, we think it is a calamity and that we're going to be condemned forever.

It's never too late to get back on track. The nature of life is to throw us off track. We are not supposed to be passengers through life; we are the pilot, continually adjusting.

Not only are your actions mostly chosen by your operating system, but your perceptual filters are also set to support the operating system.

The job of your operating system is to minimise the mental energy you have to spend. It does something called satisficing. What this means is that rather than trying to be perfectly accurate, it compromises accuracy in order to cover more ground. As much as it can, it does this by making what you see match with what you believe.

You know how politicians use facts and situations to emphasise their case? Even if they are taken completely out of context? This is exactly what your perceptual filters do. They reflect back to you, as much as they can, what you believe.

It is for this reason that arguments are generally useless in getting other people to see things your way. Whatever evidence you use, they will see it through their perspective. You know how some people just can't see what you are telling them? It doesn't matter how much you explain, or how many ways you try to tell them. This is because they can't fit it into their operating system.

To believe something, there are certain assumptions and supporting beliefs that have to be there for it to slot in. Otherwise, the information just falls flat and gets stored under miscellaneous junk. It's a bit like giving someone an ornament, without them having any shelves or cabinets to display it in.

I have a theory along these lines. I believe that when people read a book that reflects the beliefs and understanding they already have, they think it's good. If it articulates what they were thinking, but hadn't ever put it together, they think it's great. If it has beliefs they held a long time ago, or beliefs too far advanced—in other words, if it doesn't fit in with the stage they're at—they don't like it.

Whatever we believe to be good is good because that is what makes sense, given our entire Operating System. Equally, whatever we believe to be bad, right, wrong, and so on, all depends on our Operating System.

The problem with this is that we almost always have a false view of how things are. Life creates change every second, yet our Operating System shows us as constant a world as it can get away with. It is the extent of the difference between our Operating System and reality that determines the extent of the stress or happiness we experience.

In the following chapters, we will discuss how the Operating System is created and how this interacts with what happens in your life to create the emotions you feel.

❋ *Natural landmarks such as trees can indicate direction in many ways and suggest clues about the surrounding environment. Observation is key to the visible influences of the local prevailing wind.*

MAYBE

One day a wild horse turned up at a wise old man's house. At this time a horse was valuable, equivalent to a house today. All the other villagers came and congratulated him on his luck and good fortune.

"Maybe" he said.

A week later, his son was thrown trying to break the horse in. The resulting broken leg meant he could not help run the farm. This was harvest time, and all the crops would be lost. When the villagers learned of the son's accident they commiserated on his misfortune.

The wise old man would only say, "Maybe."

Source Unknown

Two weeks later, army generals came to the village, conscripting all fit young men to join in an ongoing war. The wise old man's son was the only one unaffected due to his broken leg.

14.

Journey Beyond Your Cultural Socialisation

Most of our operating system is set up in our childhood. Some of it becomes updated as we grow and are capable of understanding more. We learn that Father Christmas doesn't really bring us our presents, that adults don't know everything, and that a hundred and one other things we once believed aren't true. However, there are still many, many beliefs that never get changed, because we have never had the time, or reason, to consciously think about them.

Therefore, the socialisation process—what Freud called the introjection of society's view—is very important. Introjection means initially your parents and teachers tell you something over and over again. Eventually it becomes so ingrained that you do it to yourself in your own head. Freud used this in terms of a conscience, but I think it relates to what we believe.

This process begins with our parents or carers. We learn not just from what they consciously teach, but from their every thought, word, and action. It doesn't matter what you say, people can still pick up on your thoughts through your body language. Parents are particularly important as they provide the basic template for our operating system.

The next stage is when the child goes out to school or nursery. Here they learn that not everyone does things in the same way or thinks identically to their family. These differences demonstrate that there are choices open to them. They also learn different rules and codes of conduct for behaving in larger social groups.

This expands their operating system. What they gained from their parents and siblings were personal operating systems. Now they are being exposed to group operating systems. As it belongs to a bigger number of people, it is far broader and more inclusive.

However, it is likely to still be somewhat idiosyncratic. For example, I went to a school in London that predominantly had pupils from an Irish-Catholic background. So there were still some biased aspects of the operating system that differed from if I had gone to, say, a mostly Hindu school.

Later, we become immersed in the culture and rules of the company we work for and the industry we work in, which further influences our operating system.

The media shepherds us towards society's operating system by the slant that they put on their stories — ridiculing and savaging those who are wrong by their operating system's interpretation, and making martyrs of those who support and exemplify it.

Government then puts in place laws on the outer boundaries of society's operating system, which define society's acceptable boundaries.

It's important for us to understand how others influence us. Generally, people like to think that they make their own minds up. However, research studies consistently demonstrate how we can become swayed to conform and obey.

If you doubt the extent to which we rely on or are influenced by society, consider the following psychological studies into conformity.

In 1951, Solomon Asch studied the influence of groups on individuals. To do this, he gave a group of 7–9 participants a number of questions, such as:

Is the line on one card the same as line A, B, or C on another card?

It was set up so that the answer was fairly clear and simple. Initially the groups answered correctly for a few rounds. Here's where the experiment gets to be fun. All but one of the participants were in on the secret that this was not really a perceptual test as advertised. They all begin to answer incorrectly. The individual being studied was therefore always last, or second from last.

Film of the experiment shows the participant shaking his head and looking at his fellow group members in utter disbelief, yet when it comes around to his turn to answer, he goes along with the group. Instead of trusting his own judgement, he instead conforms to the judgement of the group. Three out of every four participants conformed to varying extents.

Remember, this occurred in tests where the answer was clearly wrong. Afterward, the experiment participants gave their reasons for conforming. Some didn't want to upset the experimenter, some figured they must have made an obscure mistake, and others began to question their judgement — *were their eyes playing tricks on them?* or *were they seeing things differently where they were sitting?* Another reason given was that they didn't want to be different from the others.

Do you see any similarity between those findings and decisions and possible views, or beliefs, you've dismissed because they don't fit in with what everyone else sees?

Asch's experiment has been carried out with many twists. One of the most interesting discoveries was the finding that there is almost no difference, in terms of influence, between three people in agreement and, say, twelve. With one other person, there is almost no influence; two, some; but three increases the outside influence a great deal.

How does this relate to situations in your life, where others disagreed or disapproved of your preferred choice?

In a group of friends, are you swayed, even unconsciously, to conform?

We each perceive reality through our perceptual filters. These relate to our individual construction of reality. This is why five people can each have a different explanation of a single event. Hence the notorious unreliability of eyewitness evidence.

From this individual construction of reality, we develop our own best response to a situation. However, when we become aware this differs from "what is normal," we begin to doubt our judgement.

During the sixties, some social psychologists became interested in how ordinary citizens in Nazi Germany were turned into cold-blooded killers, merely "following orders". A decade after Asch's studies, Stanley Milgram sought to increase our understanding of obedience.

To do so, Milgram advertised a memory test. When participants turned up, they were introduced to a young man in a lab coat and a middle-aged accountant also taking part in the experiment (who was actually one of Milgram's assistants). The researcher explained to both that the study was looking into the effects of punishment on learning. They picked a name from a hat as to who would be the teacher... rigged, of course.

The accomplice was strapped into a chair, which would deliver an electric shock every time the teacher flicked a switch.

A small shock was given to the teacher, before beginning, to convince him of the reality of the experiment.

Then he left for the teacher's room. Every time the learner made a mistake in responding or failing to respond to the teacher's question, the teacher was to give him an increasingly powerful electric shock by flicking a switch. Of course, this was all staged. The squeals from the learner's room was from a tape recording.

Initially there was little response from the Learner, which then developed into pleas to escape the experiment, to agonised screams, to refusal to continue, then to eerie silence.

If the teacher should waiver, the administrator had a script of four responses;

- Please continue
- The experiment requires that you continue
- It's absolutely essential that you continue
- You have no other choice, you must go on

There were also reassurances that the shocks, although painful, would not cause any permanent damage.

Before conducting the experiment, Milgram polled 40 psychiatrists as to what they thought would happen. They predicted less than 1% of participants would administer through to the highest, and potentially fatal, level.

What do you predict? What percentage of participants would be willing to kill someone because an experimenter tells them to, even when the fellow participant pleads to be let out?

The results shocked the scientific community. 62.5% of participants, more or less two in three, continued giving shocks up to the maximum of 450 volts.

It was not sadism, or lack of concern, on the part of the participant. Participants displayed a variety of anxious behaviours.

Some twitched, others laughed hysterically or verbally attacked the experimenter. They sweated, stuttered, trembled, groaned, bit their lips and dug their nails into their skin. Three participants had full-blown, uncontrollable seizures.

It was partly due to the effects, at the time and after the research, on participants that research like this is no longer allowed today. Many participants struggled as they realised the behaviour they were capable of.

This experiment has been conducted all over the world many times to demonstrate its reliability. Some twists have been attempted to explain why participants are so obedient.

Some claimed that because the location of the experiments was Yale University, this afforded greater authority to the experiment, and so deference to the commands.

Even when conducted from a small and run-down office, the obedience rate was still 47.5%. Perhaps the setting played a part for some participants, but there is clearly still some deeper underlying dynamic.

When the participant was in the same room the compliance rate of those who continued shocking right up to the end, dropped to 40%. A sizeable number (30%) continued, even when rather than flicking a switch, the teacher had to actually place the learner's hand on to the plate giving the shock.

When other teachers (assistants of Milgram) were present and refused to continue after a certain point, compliance reduced to just 10%.

When another person was flicking the switches, obedience rose to 92.5%.

When the experimenter left the room, obedience dropped to just 20.5%. Many only pretended to press the buttons or used a lower voltage.

What obedience and conformity both share, said Milgram, was the "…abdication of individual judgement in the face of some external social pressure…"

This is key to understanding how to improve the quality of your life. When you allow another to influence you, you have given control of your life away. Perhaps not consciously, but every decision you take or avoid taking shapes your life.

Because of the way our Operating System is created, unless we take the time to revisit the beliefs we created, or accepted, as we developed our Operating System... we are living out the beliefs of other people.

In this sense, we are mentally and spiritually cloning. The purpose of our lives can be found not in our sameness, but in our uniqueness.

Our uniqueness brings something new to the world. Our sameness adds no value, and we confuse the value we produce with our inherent value.

We conform and obey in order to please and pacify others. We need to belong to the pack and think that if others knew what we were really like, no one would want to know us. This isn't necessarily a conscious thought, but if you analyse it right down to the root of conformity, it is what you'll find.

Because of this, we strive to portray a persona that fits in — of being just one of the crowd.

Have you ever been waiting anxiously for a test result where you could have gotten anything from top mark to failure... but to stop the nail-biting, you would willingly have given up your chance for a top grade to ensure an adequate pass mark?

That is the kind of reasoning that leads people to sell out their dream in order to fit in. Being normal becomes overwhelmingly important. This is why fashions and magazines that set the tone have become increasingly popular. The intense focus on famous peoples' private lives, and the success of reality television programmes, are due to this need to find out about others.

Are they the same as me?

Am I normal?

When people find that there are many others who feel the same way as they do, much of the pressure they feel is relieved.

To some extent, we do tend to grow out of this as we get older and start to relax and just be ourselves. And this links in with research findings that show that we become happier as we age.

The rushing around like headless chickens that we often do—attempting to build success, power, status, and affection—in order to prove our value to society is mistaken.

The value we as humans create is not in following rules, ideas, and processes... it is in expanding and creating new things, new ideas, and new processes.

The people who are most valued are those who rewrite the rules. Not the people who make minor incremental improvements.

So if you feel that you lack in value, it may be because you aren't creating value—not because you are inherently lacking in value.

What most of us do is to follow the operating system we have by default. Then we become too caught up in life to even consider that we may not be thinking for ourselves. We look around and think that the fact that we lack self-esteem, motivation, success, happiness, and so on is because of a fault in us.

We look for all the ways in which we are broken. As we tune into that wavelength, our perceptual filters look for evidence that we are broken and start to find it. Now we can prove that we are not worthy, and consequently we lack self-esteem.

The real problem is that as we are not thinking for ourselves, we are not adding to the world. If we revisited each belief and decided what we as an individual chose to believe, it would tune us in to the wavelength where we are most comfortable and happiest.

Then around us we would see all we need to learn, all the circumstances and people we need in order to create, whatever it is our unique talents can provide. This new idea, creation, process, or service would then expand the boundaries of the universe. We would grow and the world would grow. Then there would be no question of your value—to you or to the world.

If you look at any person who is valued, famed, and acclaimed—from pop stars to inventors to entrepreneurs to statesmen—you will notice that not one of them ever got there by being the same as everyone else. Each had the courage to stand out from the crowd, in some way, and to stand up for their beliefs. Often they will have been ridiculed by many, but in time as others came to understand their perspective, they became our heroes and heroines.

What conventional wisdom and beliefs do you disagree with? Why?

If you have solid reasons for disagreeing… and can find a better way, a better solution… dig, test your ideas, and adjust to what life shows you. You could be on the way to finding your unique message. Spread your message. Expand the world. Then you will never doubt your value ever again.

※ *Observing and reading landmarks as a group can give a wider perspective of the environment. A common mistake is to read the environment from one angle. A tree can become multiple trees from different perspectives. The difference and subtle changes can reveal information about the orientation and position.*

THE FOUR WIVES

There was a rich merchant who had four wives. He loved the fourth wife the most and adorned her with rich robes and treated her to delicacies. He took great care of her and gave her nothing but the best.

He also loved the third wife very much. He was very proud of her and always wanted to show her off to his friends. However, the merchant was always in great fear that she might run away with some other men.

He, too, loved his second wife. She was a very considerate person, always patient, and was in fact the merchant's confidante. Whenever the merchant faced some problem, he always turned to his second wife, and she would always help him out and tide him through difficult times.

Source Unknown

Now, the merchant's first wife was a very loyal partner and had made great contributions in maintaining his wealth and business, as well as taking care of the household. However, the merchant did not love the first wife, and although she loved him deeply, he hardly took notice of her.

One day, the merchant fell ill. Before long, he knew that he was going to die soon. He thought of his luxurious life and told himself, "Now I have four wives with me. But when I die, I'll be alone. How lonely I'll be!"

Thus, he asked the fourth wife, "I loved you most, endowed you with the finest clothing, and showered great care over you. Now that I'm dying, will you follow me and keep me company?"

"No way!" replied the fourth wife and she walked away without another word.

The answer cut like a sharp knife right into the merchant's heart. The sad merchant then asked the third wife, "I have loved you so much for all my life. Now that I'm dying, will you follow me and keep me company?"

"No!" replied the third wife. "Life is so good over here! I'm going to remarry when you die!"

The merchant's heart sank and turned cold.

He then asked the second wife, "I always turned to you for help and you've always helped me out. Now I need your help again. When I die, will you follow me and keep me company?"

"I'm sorry, I can't help you out this time!" replied the second wife. "At the very most, I can only send you to your grave."

The answer came like a bolt of thunder, and the merchant was devastated.

Then a voice called out: "I'll leave with you. I'll follow you no matter where you go."

The merchant looked up, and there was his first wife. She was so skinny, almost like she suffered from malnutrition. Greatly grieved, the merchant said, "I should have taken much better care of you while I could have!"

Actually, we all have four wives in our lives:

a. The fourth wife is our body. No matter how much time and effort we lavish in making it look good, it'll leave us when we die.

b. Our third wife? Our possessions, status, and wealth. When we die, they all go to others.

c. The second wife is our family and friends. No matter how closely they have been there for us when we're alive, the furthest they can stay by us is up to the grave.

d. The first wife is, in fact, our soul, often neglected in our pursuit of material, wealth, and sensual pleasure.

Guess what? It is actually the only thing that follows us wherever we go. Perhaps it's a good idea to cultivate and strengthen it now rather than to wait until we're on our deathbed to lament

15.

Nurture Your Emotional Health

Everything in life, when you boil it down to its sub-atomic level, is just energy. This energy is the force of life. This force creates and connects everything. By definition, nothing can exist without it or separate from it.

The history of mankind has been a debate over what this force is called or wants. Today some call it God, in various languages, or the evolutionary force or life force. It doesn't matter because the words and interpretations are the petty details that only us humans care about.

This force of life flows through us. Our beliefs determine and shape the world that we experience.

As the life force flows through our beliefs, it creates an emotional reaction. This reaction is a message from Life, God, the Universe, Evolution, or whatever you wish to call it.

If the emotion is positive, your beliefs are allowing life to flow through you freely.

If the emotions are negative, there are one or more beliefs that are causing friction with the energy flowing through you. The specific emotion you feel is highlighting to you the beliefs that need changing in order for you to feel in tune with life.

I cannot conceive of a personal God who would directly influence the actions of individuals, or would directly sit in judgement on creatures of his own creation.

I cannot do this in spite of the fact that mechanistic causality has, to a certain extent, been placed in doubt by modern science.

My religiosity consists in a humble admiration of the infinitely superior spirit that reveals itself in the little that we, with our weak and transitory understanding, can comprehend of reality. Morality is of the highest importance – but for us, not for God.

Albert Einstein. The Human Side, 1954

Adapting your beliefs to fit in with your emotions will develop the truest and most effective Operating System. And this will lead you to the path that is perfectly designed for you to walk along.

The type of emotion will help to lead you to the source of the belief that is creating your discomfort. Emotional health or disease is created in exactly the same way as physical health or disease.

We are physically healthy when our body is in its natural state. When our body gets knocked out of balance through something toxic to it — such as pollutants, germs or even the biochemical side effects of too much stress — it starts to exhibit symptoms of being unwell. Many of the symptoms of a disease are actually the side effects of our body working to protect us.

For example, we experience a temperature as our immune system mobilises to attack the invader. The temperature is not caused by the disease, but by our body's reaction to the disease.

Happiness is the emotional equivalent of physical health. We become unhappy when we emotionally take on something that is alien to us.

When we speak or act in a way that is not really true to our essential nature, we become unhappy. We experience unhappiness in a number of ways. Sometimes it is guilt, anger, shame, or frustration; other times, it is anxiety.

All are the emotional equivalent of a disease or illness. Our emotions are not caused by events that happen to us... but by our reaction to the events that happen to us.

Our happiness and emotional health comes under attack whenever we think, speak, or act in a way that is not really true to our natural design. Just as with our physical health, we are continually attacked by many "invading aliens". These include:

– The pressure to conform to society's, groups and organisational rules.
– Expectations of ourselves, and others, to live up to certain standards.
– Fitting into pre-designed roles, which restrict, confine, and limit our expression of our true individuality.

These will attack us for as long as we continue to believe they are important. Once we get crystal clear on exactly who we are and what we are here to do, our emotional immune system becomes strong enough to make these invaders irrelevant to us—just as a healthy body, with sufficient nutritional reserves, will protect us from physical invaders.

❊ *Plants and trees can give us much help in finding direction. The tree ring method states that the heart of the tree is nearer the bark on the South side, usually with the thicker bark on North side.*

CRACKED POT

A water bearer in India had two large pots; each hung on each end of a pole, which he carried across his neck.

One of the pots had a crack in it, and while the other pot was perfect and always delivered a full portion of water at the end of the long walk from the stream to the master's house, the cracked pot arrived only half full.

For a full two years, this went on daily, with the bearer delivering only one and a half pots full of water in his master's house. Of course, the perfect pot was proud of its accomplishments, perfect to the end for which it was made.

But the poor cracked pot was ashamed of its own imperfection, and miserable that it was able to accomplish only half of what it had been made to do. After two years of what it perceived to be a bitter failure, it spoke to the water bearer one day by the stream.

Source Unknown

"I am ashamed of myself, and I want to apologise to you."

"Why?" asked the bearer. "What are you ashamed of?"

"I have been able, for these past two years, to deliver only half my load because this crack in my side causes water to leak out all the way back to your master's house.

Because of my flaws, you have to do all of this work, and you don't get full value from your efforts," the pot said.

The water bearer felt sorry for the old cracked pot, and in his compassion he said, "As we return to the master's house, I want you to notice the beautiful flowers along the path."

Indeed, as they went up the hill, the old cracked pot took notice of the sun warming the beautiful wild flowers on the side of the path, and this cheered it some. But at the end of the trail, it still felt bad because it had leaked out half its load, and so again it apologised to the bearer for its failure.

The bearer said to the pot, "Did you notice that there were flowers only on your side of your path, but not on the other pot's side?

That's because I have always known about your flaw, and I took advantage of it. I planted flower seeds on your side of the path, and every day while we walk back from the stream, you've watered them. For two years I have been able to pick these beautiful flowers to decorate my master's table. Without you being just the way you are, he would not have this beauty to grace his house."

Each of us has our own unique flaws. We are all cracked pots. But it is the cracks and flaws we each have that make our lives together so very interesting and rewarding.

Tap the cracks in those around you to make flowers. You've just got to take each person for what they are, and look for the good in them. There is a lot of good out there. There is a lot of good in all of us!

Blessed are the flexible, for they shall not be bent out of shape.

Remember to give to and appreciate all the different people in your life (even if they forget your name at first), and they will reciprocate, and come to appreciate and like you. If it hadn't been for the cracked pots in my life, it would have been pretty boring... and I wouldn't be were I am today!

16.

Understand Your Personality Style

Have you ever been dumbstruck by the way your partner or friend could take something so calmly, while you were boiling with rage?

Or were you the calm one that couldn't understand why they were so worked up?

Here's why.

I don't really like to categorise people into specific groups. I'm not sure if you see people like that because that's what you're looking for (the wavelength you are tuning into) or because that's how they are. However, sometimes that's the easiest way to understand patterns of behaviours.

What I have noticed is that there are two types of people.

Sometimes one person can switch between the two roles. One group I call the Structurers. These perhaps relate closely to introverts. Structurers tend to be more detached, and therefore they can be more analytical and see things with greater clarity.

The second group, I call Enhancers. This relates to extroverts. Enhancers are deeply attached; they feel things far more vividly. As a result, they are far more dramatic and bring more colour—more drama and excitement to situations.

Both groups need each other. Enhancers exaggerate what is going on. This enables Structurers to see what can be changed more easily, as it magnifies details for them. Structurers provide the detail and the foundations that provide the stage for Enhancers to bring to life far more vividly.

There is no better example of the way Structurers and Enhancers work together than in entertainment. The directors, cameramen, casting agents, and so on keep a more detached view, holding onto the bigger picture and making the details fit together perfectly.

Meanwhile the actors, actresses, dancers, singers, and so on concentrate all their focus on portraying more and more emotional depth.

The result is a believable and gripping structure that holds attention, building up to the peak emotional scenes and a depth of emotion that moves audiences to tears.

Neither is better than the other. They just play different roles to reach the same goal.

Next time you see the Drama Queen or the Insensitive Oaf in your life, remember their role in either exaggerating to highlight, or in detaching to analyse. By listening to others and honestly sharing your views, you'll get so many more insights and perspectives that life becomes so much more dimensional, and so you'll see many choices in life. Then all of your life becomes a choice.

❅ *Silphium laciniatum (compass plants) tend to align their foliage in a northerly and southerly direction, presenting the minimum amount of surface area to the intense heat of the midday Sun.*

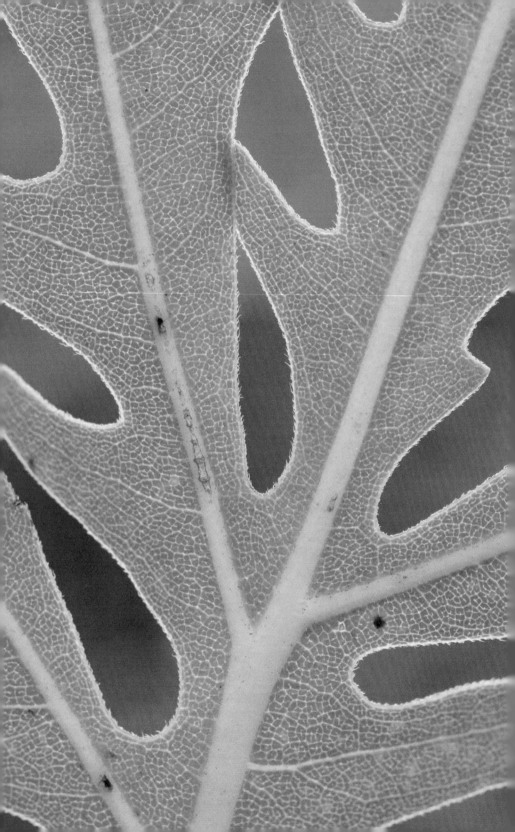

THE BRICK AND THE JAG

About ten years ago, a young and very successful executive named Josh was travelling down a Chicago neighbourhood street. He was going a bit too fast in his sleek black 12-cylinder Jaguar XKE, which was only two months old.

He was watching for kids darting out from between parked cars and slowed down when he thought he saw something. As his car passed, no child darted out, but a brick sailed out and—WHUMP!—it smashed into the Jag's shiny black side door! SCREECH…! Brakes slammed! Gears ground into reverse, and tires madly spun the Jaguar back to the spot from where the brick had been thrown. Josh jumped out of the car, grabbed the kid, and pushed him up against a parked car. He shouted at the kid, "What was that all about and who are you? Just what the heck are you doing?!"

Source Unknown

Building up a head of steam, he went on, "That's my new Jag, that brick you threw is gonna cost you a lot of money. Why did you throw it?"

"Please, mister, please… I'm sorry! I didn't know what else to do!" pleaded the youngster. "I threw the brick because no one else would stop!" Tears were dripping down the boy's chin as he pointed around the parked car. "It's my brother, mister," he said. "He rolled off the curb and fell out of his wheelchair and I can't lift him up." Sobbing, the boy asked the executive, "Would you please help me get him back into his wheelchair? He's hurt and he's too heavy for me."

Moved beyond words, the young executive tried desperately to swallow the rapidly swelling lump in his throat. Straining, he lifted the young man back into the wheelchair and took out his handker -chief and wiped the scrapes and cuts, checking to see that everything was going to be OK. He then watched the younger brother push him down the side walk toward their home.

It was a long walk back to the sleek, black, shining, 12 cylinder Jaguar XKE — a long and slow walk. Josh never did fix the side door of his Jaguar. He kept the dent to remind him not to go through life so fast that someone has to throw a brick at him to get his attention…. Some bricks are softer than others. Feel for the bricks of life coming at to you. For all the negative things we have to say to ourselves, God has positive answers.

17.

Manage Your Emotions

We generally think of our emotions as being directly caused by events. "You made me feel...", "It was the... that made me feel...". This is the thinking that traps us as powerless victims.

There is no such thing as a stressful situation. Only stressful thoughts. The same situation can be an opportunity for great achievement or great anxiety. It all depends on how you perceive and respond to it. The situation in itself is neutral.

Any pressure, stress, frustration, disappointment, or anger we feel is caused only by the mental frameworks we use to see and evaluate life through.

We only feel these emotions when we have a time frame or deadline that has to be met. Or when there is an image of the way something must match up to. Take away the mental constructions—and they are only constructed through your beliefs—and all you have is life, happening in its own perfect way.

No one else can ever make you feel anything. Events happen, life just is. We feel emotions in response to our thoughts about things.

The actual events are neutral. If you get a promotion... if you win the lottery... if your football team wins— these are neutral events.

But because you have attached value to these events as being good—you think of them as being good. To the people you pass in the street, they mean nothing.

Nothing is good or bad. Only thinking makes it so.

William Shakespeare

The nature of the way we perceive the world and our way of thinking economically, causes us to forget this. For this reason, we often have difficulty in understanding others and how they feel.

Life is like a torch. It flows through us and shines onto our beliefs. The projection is what we think of as the outside world. It is actually what we choose to see of the outside world. If you change your beliefs, it will be like changing radio stations, and as you tune into different information... you will see a different version of reality.

At the same time, your Operating System synthesizes all the information you have on a particular situation or issue. Then in processing these through your beliefs, it determines what is good, and bad, in relation to the issue. From these, it creates a Should Vision. This is the ideal outcome from the understanding you have.

This Should Vision is key to your emotions. Whatever you feel is determined by how close your Should Vision is to reality. If they match up, you'll feel happy. The more contrast and difference that you see, the more miserable you will feel.

Stress is the tension of literally trying to pull reality into the same shape as your Should Vision.

Your emotions are your built-in guidance system. We are naturally drawn to feel good and averse to feeling bad. So when we feel bad, we are forced to try to feel better. There are three main ways to do this.

1. Many people simply try to dull down their feelings. Some with drink, drugs, work, television—anything to dull and distract themselves from feeling. The problem with this is that they are always moving away from pain, and the distractions never last for long. Meanwhile, the pain is growing greater and greater all the time.

2. More try to change the outer world. Life feels so hard, like such a struggle, when you are trying to control, influence, and change the hundreds of variables you notice. Add in the fact that there are thousands more that you cannot even see, let alone change, and you have a recipe for frustration, anger, and heartache.

3. The easiest option is the least taken. It is so much easier to change the one thing that you have complete and utter control over: your beliefs. If you change these then immediately—though you may not see it in your reality immediately—one or perhaps two changes will occur. Firstly, by changing your beliefs you have relaxed your Should Vision and so it will become more flexible. Secondly, by changing your beliefs, you may also have changed your perceptual filters—thereby changing the way that the world looks.

In a few hundred years, when the history of our time will be written from a long-term perspective, it is likely that the most important event historians will see is not technology, not the internet, not e-commerce.

It is an unprecedented change in the human condition.

For the first time – literally – substantial and rapidly growing numbers of people have choices. For the first time, they will have to manage themselves. And society is totally unprepared for it.

Peter F. Drucker

❄ *When observation cannot be used,*
other senses can be relied upon.
The heat of the Sun will be conserved
for many hours after the visible
signs have dispersed.

A PICTURE OF PEACE

There once was a king who offered a prize to the artist who would paint the best picture of peace. Many artists tried. The king looked at all the pictures, but there were only two he really liked, and he had to choose between them.

One picture was of a calm lake. The lake was a perfect mirror, for peaceful, towering mountains were all around it.

Overhead was a blue sky with fluffy white clouds. All who saw this picture thought that it was a perfect picture of peace.

The other picture had mountains, too. But these were rugged and bare. Above was an angry sky from which rain fell and in which lightening played. Down the side of the mountain tumbled a foaming waterfall. This did not look peaceful at all.

Source Unknown

But when the king looked, he saw behind the waterfall a tiny bush growing in a crack in the rock. In the bush, a mother bird had built her nest. There, in the midst of the rush of angry water, sat the mother bird on her nest... perfect peace.

Which picture do you think won the prize?

The king chose the second picture. Do you know why?

"Because," explained the king, "peace does not mean to be in a place where there is no noise, trouble, or hard work.

Peace means to be in the midst of all those things and still be calm in your heart. That is the real meaning of peace."

18.

Appreciate the Role of Disharmony and Imperfection

Generally, we go through life and think that if only life was easier... if only everyone saw and did things our way... that the world would be some kind of paradise. This is a mistake based on the idea that if the world matched up to your Should Vision it would be perfect. It is a mistake because the information that makes up your Should Vision is mistaken, false, and incomplete.

First think about this: what would be your idea of paradise? The most common vision seems to involve lying in a hammock on the most beautiful beach, having the tastiest foods and drink fed to you by the most attractive waiting staff. Every material possession only has to be reached for and everyone agrees.

There are no conflicts.

When you're feeling bruised and sore... when life seems too frantic and too harsh... this vision seems more and more seductive. Yet this wish is just as flawed as King Midas's wish to turn everything he touched into gold.

It would take only a few days to get bored with living the same day over and over again. Which is what this vision would be.

We do not really want everyone to agree with us. We only want to be able to get along with each other, even if our opinions differ. We don't want everything to just fall in our laps. We just want to know that we can steer our lives in the right direction. And that we do have a reasonable chance to achieve our goals

If you look at every aspect of life, you can see that there is never an end. There is no perfection, because with every improvement there are always further possibilities. Life is the game that never ends. The universe expands with every breath. Each creature evolves into an ever more complex and sophisticated version.

As a society, we expand from disharmony—not the kind of destructive disharmony that creates war and destruction, but the kind of disharmony that leads to progress. The disharmony that turns conventional wisdom on its head. This kind of creative friction is the force of progress and evolution. It is this that forces our society to expand to include new ideas.

When there is just one idea that everyone agrees with, there is harmony. It could also be called a trap. When there are two or more ideas, you have the ability to exercise free will and direct your own life. Wherever there are two or more ideas, there is also the possibility to synthesize the two and create new ideas. The more ideas there are, the more possibilities open up.

The problem is that we have always had a tendency to mistake others for their ideas. Rather than separating the person from the idea and feeling harmonious with the person, but not necessarily the idea, we feel that it is offensive to contradict someone.

And so we don't.

However, by superficially agreeing, even when we don't, we create a split deep inside of us. The split grows into a chasm and causes us to feel frustration. This creates a resentment against the other—for no other reason than that our pretence has made us feel bad. Then when we feel sufficiently angry, we'll snap. But by now as we have identified the person as being tied to the idea, we now experience disharmony with the individual, rather than the idea.

It is all based on a fundamental misunderstanding. People are not the ideas that they speak. Any idea spoken is just a snapshot of that person's thoughts. Now, it is true that due to economy of thought, many people in our world do not pay much attention to the ideas they hold and so don't change them very often. However, the person is still not the idea. Yet our Operating System, using as little mental energy as possible, sometimes does link them together in the images it uses to represent them.

If we free ourselves from this mental shortcut, we are able to discuss ideas freely without offence. This is the greatest way that we can evolve—by sharing ideas and putting all the pieces together in our own way to create our own picture. When we are able to truly share our thoughts and ideas, without fear of offending others, then we are able to find ourselves. Read on to find out why...

☀ *Many species of insects and animals have an inbuilt awareness when navigating and finding direction, utilising their surroundings, the Sun, visual landmarks, and the Earth's electromagnetic field. Bees are intriguing solar navigators that orientate themselves relative to the Sun.*

SOCRATES AND THE SECRET

A young man asked Socrates the secret of success. Socrates told the young man to meet him near the river the next morning. They met. Socrates asked the young man to walk with him into the river. When the water got up to their necks, Socrates took the young man by surprise and swiftly ducked him into the water.

The boy struggled to get out, but Socrates was strong and kept him there until the boy started turning blue. Socrates pulled the boy's head out of the water, and the first thing the young man did was to gasp and take a deep breath of air.

Socrates asked him, "What did you want the most when you were there?" The boy replied, "Air." Socrates said, "That is the secret of success! When you want success as badly as you wanted the air, then you will get it!" There is no other secret.

19.

Identify Your True Self

All of life is so, so simple. Yet the entire history of humanity has been of an ever-growing complexity. The result is that we sit here with few people having a strong sense of identity... and social problems that have become so tangled that no one seems to understand how to untangle them.

Increasingly over the last couple of decades, more and more people have been searching for a deeper sense of identity. There is nowhere to go to find yourself. The answer to who you are is simple. You only have to look into the mirror and say what you see.

But any slight deviation from the complete and absolute truth—when you tell someone, "No, you don't look fat in that," "Yes, everything will work out fine," when that is not what you believe—each causes a split in the mirror.

Every time that you tell a lie, whether your intention behind it was good or bad, you create a split in your internal reality. A lie is a denial of who you are.

Once you have told a lie, you then have to keep hold of the truth in your mind; but at the same time, you have to hold onto the alternate reality.

Now your mental energy has been split in two.

Add to this the fact that many lies need other lies to maintain the original. Each then further divides your mental realities.

Sometimes people will tell two, three, or even more versions of the same event to different audiences. This then divides their mental energy, to maintain however many different stories they have told. Plus, on top of that, there is the additional worry of being found out. The result is similar to the effects of being schizophrenic.

If you take every internal conflict between one part of you that wants to do X and another that wants to do Y and add to these every lie you have allowed to be interpreted from your responses—this determines how shattered your mirror is.

Since the mirror is shattered, it is difficult to see who you are. Am I the me in this fragment, or that? Until you are whole and integrated—expressing your deepest ideal self, in every situation—you cannot, and neither can anyone else, know your authentic self.

As a result, you do not add to the world. You do not create the value that you would by sharing your unique message, and so you turn yourself into a commodity. To others you look bland, and therefore, just like many others. Therefore, neither they nor you can see anything special about you. And so they don't value you as highly as they could—and neither do you.

The key to life is integrity, in every sense of the word. Generally we think of integrity as meaning honesty. What it actually means is the integration of everything you think, say, and do. When you are fully integrated and congruent, then who you are is no longer a question, but a statement. In the meantime, all the searching in the world won't help you to find yourself.

The five colours blind the eye.
The five tones deafen the ear.
The five flavours dull the taste.
Racing and hunting madden the mind.
Precious things lead one astray.
Therefore the sage is guided by what he
feels and not by what he sees.
He lets go of that and chooses this.

Lao Tsu

☀ *It has long being suggested that birds have an in-built compass: the ability to navigate by magnetism. Birds are believed to be sensitive to the Earth's magnetic field, the axial direction, strength and dip.*

THE CRICKET!

A Native American and his friend were in downtown New York City, walking near Times Square in Manhattan. It was during the noon lunch hour and the streets were filled with people. Cars were honking their horns, taxicabs were squealing around corners, sirens were wailing, and the sounds of the city were almost deafening.

Suddenly, the Native American said, "I hear a cricket."

His friend said, "What? You must be crazy. You couldn't possibly hear a cricket in all of this noise!"

"No, I'm sure of it," the Native American said, "I heard a cricket."

"That's crazy," said the friend.

The Native American listened carefully for a moment, and then walked across the street to a big cement planter where some shrubs

Source Unknown

were growing. He looked into the bushes, beneath the branches, and sure enough, he located a small cricket. His friend was utterly amazed.

"That's incredible," said his friend. "You must have super–human ears!"

"No," said the Native American. "My ears are no different from yours. It all depends on what you're listening for."

"But that can't be!" said the friend. "I could never hear a cricket in this noise."

"Yes, it's true," came the reply. "It depends on what is really important to you. Here, let me show you."

He reached into his pocket, pulled out a few coins, and discreetly dropped them on the side walk

And then, with the noise of the crowded street still blaring in their ears, they noticed every head within twenty feet turn and look to see if the money that tinkled on the pavement was theirs.

"See what I mean?" asked the Native American. "It all depends on what's important to you."

20.

Create an Underlying Sense of Purpose To Your Life

There are many theories, but no one actually knows why, or how, we evolved the more powerful capacity for conscious thought. Somewhere along the evolutionary path, though, we did. We became able to predict eventualities and to co-operatively prepare for these possible outcomes.

To predict an outcome requires a framework of understanding far beyond just what might happen. It often involves making a leap of imagination derived from certain facts we know. Sooner or later our experience tells us whether our imaginative leap was accurate or not.

Now, what that jump in brain evolution did was enable us to think in a more complex way. Our thoughts went beyond the hard-wired instincts that we share with animals into wondering why. This is why we have evidence of worship from palaeolithic cavemen, but none of animals worshipping a God.

Every question requires an answer, and the question why ultimately leads to a variety of explanations that can be called religions. This is why I say that God may have made man, but man certainly made God.

Joseph Campbell puts it far more eloquently than I could; *God is a metaphor for that which transcends all levels of intellectual thought. It's as simple as that.*

Consider the early cavemen and women trying to create a sense of order from the patterns they saw in their life.

Why their prey sometimes turned up and others it didn't? Why their efforts were sometimes helped and sometimes hindered by weather and luck?

Given the fact that they had no scientific knowledge to inform them, they were likely to fill in the gaps in their knowledge with superstition and magical stories. Noticing that they preyed on some animals and those on others, it is likely that they believed in a hierarchy of importance.

Therefore, it must have seemed logical that there was someone, or something invisible, that preyed upon them. Taking their kin when it chose, punishing them with poor weather, or healing them and providing favourable weather and food.

Just as a subservient dog will try to placate its owner, our ancestors attempted to placate the gods. Immediately, man had created a higher purpose beyond survival. The more they learned about the world around them, the more sophisticated their story of their place in the world and their relation to God became.

Societies came and went. Languages changed. But every institution, every word and every custom, became stained with this belief. And so today it doesn't matter whether you are religious or not; you still, through the language you use and the socialisation process, operate through a cognitive framework that fears the wrath of God. Not consciously perhaps, but analyse your thoughts to their roots and you'll find some evidence for this.

Through history there have been many wise and great individuals who transcended these limitations. People such as Jesus, Buddha, Mohammad, Lao Tsu, and Confucius. These individuals have explained life in the language of their own times and culture, in ways most appropriate for their peers. But words are so limiting.

The more that you focus on something, the more details you see of it. This is why Eskimos have many words for different types of snow, while we only have the one word. These visionaries tried to use words understood from common experiences to explain experiences and concepts others couldn't relate to, and so did not have words for.

Add to this the fact that our capacity to understand is limited by our willingness. Life could not be any simpler. But if we are emotionally unwilling to drop some of our beliefs, then it becomes far harder to intellectually understand—sometimes impossible.

As a result, the followers often hang onto the literal words rather than the spirit of the message. Look at how many varying interpretations there are of different religious books to see how open words are to misunderstanding. Often many decades later these works were written down. Through the centuries, they have been taken out of all context and translated through hundreds of languages, changed by misinterpretation, or outright manipulation, and then are expected to make perfect sense to us. Today two or more people will quote the exact same passage in defence or opposition to the same action at the same time.

Even before the written form of these words appeared, there was a general consensus as to an agreed code of conduct. Yet no one was quite sure of the rules. Indeed, even today no one is certain.

Therefore, we felt the need to elevate certain people who seemed to know.

This began with tribal and religious leaders. As our society has become more complex, it has extended into experts on every area of life. There are people who claim to know the rules about areas as varied as social etiquette to interior design.

The problem comes not in listening and using these experts' advice, but in substituting it for our own. Specialists can save you years in gaining insight without trial and error, but that knowledge must fit in with your overall strategy and approach to life or you've just copied part of someone else's blueprint.

An agreed code of conduct now gave us a standard to judge ourselves against. From here on, our value became evaluated against these external standards. And here began the centuries old conflict between society and the individual.

As an individual, you have certain wants, needs, and actions that may help you to further along your chosen path.

Yet everyone else — from your family and friends to your employer or employees and government — wants you to do, or believe, certain things. Sometimes it's just because from their limited understanding, they believe that your life would be better if you believed or did certain things. Other times, such as the millions of soldiers who've lost their lives in battle, it's because they believe sacrificing you is worth it for themselves or others.

In reality, the sacrifice of your time, free will, or even your life is no more necessary than the human sacrificial rites we once performed. It is all based on a belief that the world is not expansive enough for us all to be ourselves. A belief that there is some Supreme Being somewhere who needs us all to conform to his/her plan.

Today we have enough scientific knowledge to override this view. Everything science tells us, from genetics to quantum physics to biochemistry, all indicates that order and perfection is built into the system. The world is not a random chaotic mixture. It is a perfect blend that has an inevitable result.

The expansion in size — in complexity and understanding of ourselves and of the universe — is guaranteed. We don't have to distort ourselves to fit in. Instead, it's all the better if we don't fit in. Then the world has to grow to accommodate us.

The sacrifice strategy doesn't work. One of the most common areas we see this used is by women in the homemaker role. Society, in relatively recent times, has always told them that they must forget themselves in order to devote themselves to their family. Then their daughters can grow up to sacrifice themselves for their daughters, and so on.

So who ever gets to live?

The cycle perpetuates itself, until we have a whole family line of what could-have-beens.

Many people take an attack on the sacrifice strategy to be a call for everyone to do whatever they want at any expense. Wherever the sacrifice strategy is used, the view is that someone must lose — either the sacrificer or the person or organisation the sacrifice is made for.

Wrong.

It is only looking through the old world view that this is true. As Einstein said: *"The significant problems we face cannot be solved at the same level of thinking we were at when we created them."*

The situation is a challenge for all concerned to grow. If you sacrifice, it is because you did not act on the prod life has given you to grow, and find a solution that doesn't require anyone to lose. And at the same time, you have also denied those others from making the same growth.

The world is expansive enough for everyone to get what they need. Yet what they want is often not what they need, because their understanding of life is flawed. And so sometimes the fact that you may not sacrifice yourself to fit in with their plan forces them to rethink. This may then be the catalyst for them to create a newer and more refined plan.

From birth, society has trained us to put the good of others before our own needs—to care more for others than for ourselves. Anything other than this is selfish, uncaring, and any other manipulative words that can be used to get you to fall into line.

The problem is that it isn't possible to care more for others than for ourselves. We can never feel anyone else's pain more acutely than our own—however empathic we are. And the less cared for, the less loved we feel... the less capacity we have to love.

So from birth we have a continual fight: a fight between the external world, that tells us over and over again that it knows more than us and we must be bad to not agree with it—and our body, our instincts, and intuitive knowledge that screams to us that the world is wrong and what we are doing is wrong.

In the face of such numerical and historical support from the external world, almost all of us give in and dismiss our instincts.

Then we tell ourselves that we must be bad. So we hide our real feelings and put on a social mask. Although everyone else is going through the same conflict, the fear that anyone else may think we are odd or bad means that we look at others and think, *They're coping, I should be able to.*

So we trick ourselves into believing that we are really bad and so we need to be controlled. Therefore we need more rules, more regulation, more constraints, and less trust. The debate goes back at least as far as historical records show, and probably much further.

The result is that we have been disconnected from our own source of wisdom and insight, from each other and from the universe.

The view that we need religion and laws to keep us all from raping and pillaging our neighbours supports the very institutions that created the view in the first place. We need order, they say, or we'll all behave like animals. Yet animals have their own order. It may not fit in with ours, but it is an order that makes sense for them.

Contrast that to the order we have artificially perpetuated. Year after year, newspapers scream that the crime rate is increasing... mental illnesses is increasing... loneliness is increasing... more powerful weapons of mass destruction are being created... more of the world is being destroyed... more species are being made extinct... more of the world's resources are being depleted.

The planet has been systematically and ruthlessly raped and pillaged. Not by animals, savages, or by rotten individuals... but by society attempting to maintain "the Rules".

It's time to wake up and recognise that we backed the wrong side. It's not our instincts or our inner badness that are at the root of the problem. It's wanting to have life conform with the expectations of a stale system. And it's our instincts that hold the key to growing it into a more enlightened form. Without our higher wisdom, just like a tree that's growth is blocked, we grow gnarled and knotty.

You see, there's a reason for our instincts and desires. And when we purely act on these, there isn't a problem. However, when we repress and suppress what we really feel and want, those wants and feelings get distorted into something that can be seen as bad.

Now from this point on, you can be 100% responsible for what you believe.

Since you are responsible for what you believe... you must also be responsible for what you say and do.

If you are responsible for what you think, say and do... you must also be responsible for the results that happen in your life.

❋ *True north is a fixed point and refers to the geographic North Pole. Magnetic north shifts with time and refers to the pole of the Earth's magnetic field.*

Earth's magnetic field is the geomagnetic field that extends from the Earth's inner core to where it meets the solar wind, a stream of energetic particles emanating from the Sun.

I AM ME AND I'M OKAY

I am Me. In all the world, there is no one else exactly like me. Everything that comes out of me is authentically mine, because I alone chose it—I own everything about me: my body, my feelings, my mouth, my voice, all my actions, whether they be to others or myself.

I own my fantasies, my dreams, my hopes, my fears. I own my triumphs and successes, all my failures and mistakes. Because I own all of me, I can become intimately acquainted with me. By so doing, I can love me and be friendly with all my parts.

I know there are aspects about myself that puzzle me, and other aspects that I do not know—but as long as I am friendly and loving to myself, I can courageously and hopefully look for solutions to the puzzles and ways to find out more about me.

I am me, and I am Okay.
From Self Esteem by Virginia Satira

However I look and sound, whatever I say and do, and whatever I think and feel at a given moment in time is authentically me. If later some parts of how I looked, sounded, thought, and felt turn out to be unfitting, I can discard that which is unfitting, keep the rest, and invent something new for that which I discarded.

I can see, hear, feel, think, say, and do. I have the tools to survive, to be close to others, to be productive, and to make sense and order out of the world of people and things outside of me. I own me, and therefore, I can engineer me.

21.

Gain Clarity, Courage, and Competence

In the last chapter, we spoke about the importance of integrity, in the sense of all of you being integrated. Once every part of you is aligned and working in the same direction, you will become many times more effective and powerful.

The only thing that is separating you from everything you want is lack of clarity. If you stop and analyse all the problems you'll ever face, you'll discover they come in one of three categories:

- One is a lack of clarity, not knowing exactly what the problem is and therefore not being certain what to do.
- Two is a lack of courage to believe in your own solution or your ability to carry it out.
- Three is a lack of competence to carry it out effectively. If you go even deeper, you will see that courage is derived from understanding what needs to be done and the risks involved.

Once these risks are minimised and you see the possible consequences of not acting outweigh the reduced risks of acting, you'll find the courage to act. So courage also comes from clarity.

Likewise, competence is the ability to recognise exactly what needs to be done. Many people use the old story of a plumber. who after tapping a pipe with a hammer, charged £100. When challenged for an itemised bill, he wrote an invoice for £5 for tapping the pipe and £95 for knowing where to tap. The more knowledge and experience we have, the quicker, more accurate, and effective we become. So competence also originates from clarity.

Our barrier to clarity is the shattered–mirror syndrome. The clarity with which you see is a reflection of how integrated you are. We tend to tune into different frequencies, dependant on where we are and who we are with. Therefore, we see parts of one frequency, parts of another, and so on. All are fragments of different worlds. So they do not make up a complete and clear picture.

Slugs perceive the world by taking a snapshot of what's around them every three seconds. So if you put something in front of them and took it away in the three seconds they weren't paying attention, it would seem the thing has disappeared. With this type of perception, it is very difficult to separate cause and effect.

This is the effect that the shattered–mirror syndrome has on us. We see something, then we alter our perceptual frequency to fit in with the situation we are in; and so when we return to the previous perceptual frequency. we can't see clearly enough to make sense of what has happened. Once you consistently tune in to your natural wavelength, you will get consistent perceptions of the world. This consistency of perception enables you to get a clearer picture of life.

When you are always tuned into your natural wavelength, you will always think, speak, and act consistently with the core of what you really are. Then it is clear for everyone to really know who you are. But when you jump from one thing to another depending on the context you're in, no one can know who you are—not even you.

Achieving this clarity is the secret to mastering your life. With it, you will always know what to do, how to do it, and you'll know the situation well enough to have the courage to act. Read on to find out how to achieve greater clarity.

❋ *Lodestone, meaning 'course stone' or 'leading stone'.*

A lodestone is a naturally magnetised piece of the mineral magnetite. Ancient people first discovered the natural property of magnetism in lodestone. Pieces of lodestone, suspended so they could turn, were used as the first magnetic compasses.

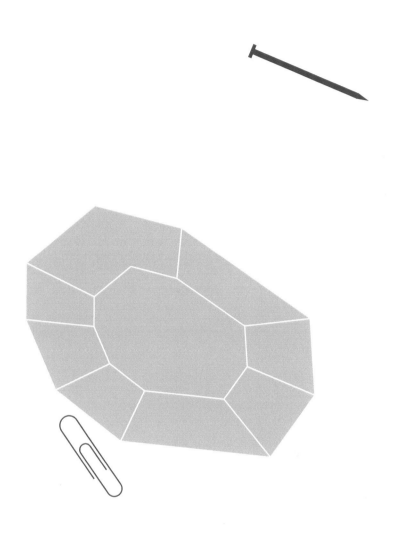

EVERY MORNING

Every morning in Africa a gazelle wakes up and knows that it will have to outrun the fastest lion or it will be killed.

And every morning in Africa, a lion wakes up and knows that it will have to outrun the slowest gazelle or it will starve to death.

So, in Africa, it doesn't matter if you are the lion or the gazelle. When that sun comes up, you had better be running.

Dan Montano

22.

Deepen the Three Key Relationships In Your Life

There are three keys to life. If you manage these, they will open you up to all the riches you ever want in life. Here are the three keys:

- Your relationship with yourself.
- Your relationship with others.
- Your relationship with the symbols of success.

Your relationship with yourself is the key to all the joy that your inner world can bring.

Your relationship with others is the key to all the joy and pleasure that people can bring into your life.

Your relationship with the symbols of success is the key to all the joy and pleasure our planet can bring.

It all starts with your relationship with yourself. It's this that sets the wavelength that you tune into. The information you take in and the way you process this information determines what you will say and do. This determines the success of your relationships with others and how successful you will be.

Of course, it is possible to be materially successful without feeling comfortable with yourself. For some people, that's what drives them to have to be successful. But that kind of success is empty.

So ultimately everything depends upon your relationship with yourself...

❋ *The revolution of the Earth,*
in conjunction with the tilt of
the axis and the Sun, means
that throughout the orbit —
day to night, summer to winter
— we experience a change in the
amount of light and heat.

THE TWO WOLVES

There was Grandfather. His little grandson often came in the evenings to sit at his knee and ask the many questions that children ask. One day the grandson came to Grandfather with a look of anger on his face.

Grandfather said, "Come, sit, tell me what has happened today." The child sat and leaned his chin on Grandfather's knee. Looking up into the wrinkled, nut-brown face and the kind dark eyes, the child's anger turned to quiet tears.

The boy said, "I went to the town today, with Father, to trade the furs he has collected over the past several months. I was happy to go, because father said that since I had helped him with the trapping, I could get something for me... something that I wanted.

Source Unknown

I was so excited to be in the trading post. I have not been there before. I looked at many things and finally found a metal knife! It was small, but good size for me, so Father got it for me."

Here the boy laid his head against Grandfather's knee and became silent.

Grandfather softly placed his hand on the boy's raven hair and said, "And then what happened?"

Without lifting his head, the boy said, "I went outside to wait for Father, and to admire my new knife in the sunlight.

Some town boys came by and saw me. They got all around me and started saying bad things. They called me dirty and stupid and said that I should not have such a fine knife.

The largest of these boys pushed me back and I fell over one of the other boys. I dropped my knife and one of them snatched it up and they all ran away laughing."

Here, the boy's anger returned. "I hate them. I hate them all!"

Grandfather, with eyes that have seen too much, lifted his grandson's face so his eyes looked into the boy's.

Grandfather said, "Let me tell you a story. I, too, at times, have felt a great hate for those that have taken so much, with no sorrow for what they do. But hate wears you down, and does not hurt your enemy. It is like taking poison and wishing your enemy would die.

I have struggled with these feelings many times. It is as if there are two wolves inside me; one is white and one is black.

The White Wolf is good and does no harm. He lives in harmony with all around him and does not take offence when no offence was intended. But it will only fight when it is right to do so, and in the right way.

But the Black Wolf is full of anger. The littlest thing will set him into a fit of temper. He fights everyone, all the time, for no reason. He cannot think because his anger and hate are so great.

It is helpless anger, for his anger will change nothing.

Sometimes it is hard to live with these two wolves inside me, for both of them try to dominate my spirit."

The boy looked intently into Grandfather's eyes and asked, "Which one wins, Grandfather?"

Grandfather smiled and said, "The one I feed."

23.

Develop Unconditional Self-Esteem

I have read thousands of books, articles, and message-board posts advising how to boost your self-esteem. And most of them are the equivalent of painting a house that is about to collapse.

Keep yourself busy. Get out more. Achieve something. Write three good things about yourself. Buy new clothes and make an effort with your appearance. Almost no one takes the time to think what the problem really is:

- It doesn't matter if you have more money than Bill Gates.
- It doesn't matter if you have more friends than a Hollywood casting director.
- It doesn't matter if you look like Brad Pitt or J Lo.
- It doesn't matter if you have a book bigger than War and Peace filled with nice things about yourself.

These things still won't give you self-esteem — not the kind of lasting self-esteem that you'll maintain, whatever happens.

They may make you feel better. They will probably give you more confidence. But confidence is an entirely different thing from self-esteem—although most people don't seem to realise it.

But in your mind, there will always be a nagging little doubt. A little voice that creeps up on you.

"What if you lose your money?"...

"What if you fail next time?"...

"What if your friends don't like you any more?"...

"What if you get it wrong?"

So actually, the only thing these will bring you is a good feeling for as long as they last—and a feeling of insecurity in case they don't last.

Why won't they change your self-esteem?

Because self-esteem really has nothing to do with anything other than your own judgement of how worthy you are. These are how Webster's and WordNet define self-esteem.

Self-esteem \Self`-es*teem"\, n. The holding a good opinion of one's self; self-complacency.

Source: Webster's Revised Unabridged Dictionary (1913)

Self-esteem n.
1. A feeling of pride in yourself [syn: {self-pride}]
2. The quality of being worthy of esteem or respect; "it was beneath his dignity to cheat"; "showed his true dignity when under pressure" [syn: {dignity}, {self-respect}, {self-regard}]

Source: WordNet (r) 2.0

Note that nowhere does it mention that your self-esteem depends to any extent on what others think. However, dependency is built into our biology. We are the most prematurely born creatures, being basically dependent for the first 12 or 14 years of our existence. This causes us to seek approval, trust in authority, and fear retribution. So what typically happens is that we depend on others for our needs, and our judgement becomes only a reflection of the judgements of other people. And then self-esteem and happiness becomes out of our own hands, dependent on what other people think and do.

Therefore, developing independence of thought and a spirit of self-determination is an essential step to creating a stable and unconditional sense of self-esteem.

Achieving this means going beyond society's indoctrination and developing a deeper understanding of the world and how you see yourself fitting into it. All the details and the landscape of your life will change with the passage of time. Losses will happen, friendships will end, looks will fade, and successes will pass. But the only thing that is constant and will always be with you... is you.

So to really develop a belief in yourself that doesn't depend on everything going right — a belief that will comfort and support you whatever happens in life — you need to understand exactly where you fit into the grand scheme of the universe.

It's not as snappy as the usual kind of three steps you usually see. It's not as much fun as going out more. Nor is it as obvious as achieving more.

But by developing a philosophy that guides you, you'll prevent ever being back in the same situation again.

You get to choose what is true. Your imagination is like a catalogue. All you can imagine is possible; you get to choose what you bring to life through your belief.

Self-esteem means the value that you place on yourself. So many people are going through life, blaming their parents, their exes, and anyone else in the firing line for their low self-esteem.

And books, magazines articles, and so on are so outwardly focused that they perpetuate the myth. They assume self-esteem must be a reflection of the extent the outward world values you.

The world can only value what it sees, though. And it only gets to see what is the tip of a massive iceberg. Whatever you have achieved or haven't achieved, there is far, far more potential for the future.

We live in a physical body, but that is not who we are. The body is a vehicle for us to express our message and display our beliefs.

The body needs the essence of us to power it. However, we are too expansive to fit into our body. So what we can't fit in stays outside; this is sometimes called the Higher Self, Daemon, Genius, or Aura, depending on your spiritual framework. The more of you that you allow in, the more energy, strength, and motivation you will feel.

The extent that you deny yourself is the emptiness that you feel. And in feeling that emptiness, it doesn't matter what you say or do for others. Your words and actions will be stained with bitterness, frustration, and anger.

When you allow yourself to let in all that you are, you will soon overflow with love and joy. You will not then be capable of not helping others. Everything you think, say, and do will become stained with your love and joy. People will feel uplifted just by being in your presence.

If you look at what made Jesus so popular, it was not his words. Throughout history there have been many eloquent and articulate speakers. It was the fact that his love for everyone overflowed from him to everywhere his attention spread. Yet we have always looked at his example, but through our limited understanding, the assumptions that we made were that he must have been directing his focus outside and thereby neglecting himself. Hence the myth of sacrifice.

Wrong.

Jesus created an unlimited source of love and energy by loving himself first. He did this by taking time to be on his own, e.g. 40 days and nights in the desert.

Despite having more opponents than followers, Jesus did not take their opinion on his value. He instead looked within, and as his own source, accepted himself as he was and loved himself.

This enabled him to relax his beliefs and therefore access unlimited energy, wisdom, and insight.

❋ *The shape and alignment of visual landmarks can yield directional clues. The southern side of landmarks in the northern hemisphere often experience a greater variation of temperatures than the northern side, made visible in the mountains by the varying height of the snow line, leading to greater impact and erosive force on the south side.*

THE POWER OF A FRIEND

One day, when I was a freshman in high school, I saw a kid from my class was walking home from school. His name was Kyle.

It looked like he was carrying all of his books. I thought to myself, "Why would anyone bring home all his books on a Friday? He must really be a nerd."

I had quite a weekend planned (parties and a football game with my friends the next afternoon), so I shrugged my shoulders and went on. As I was walking, I saw a bunch of kids running toward him. They ran at him, knocking all his books out of his arms and tripping him so he landed in the dirt.

His glasses went flying, and I saw them land in the grass about ten feet from him. He looked up and I saw this terrible sadness in his eyes. My heart went out to him.

Source Unknown

So I jogged over to him, and as he crawled around looking for his glasses, I saw a tear in his eye. As I handed him his glasses, I said, "Those guys are jerks. They really should get lives."

He looked at me and said, "Hey, thanks!" There was a big smile on his face. It was one of those smiles that showed real gratitude.

I helped him pick up his books, and asked him where he lived.

As it turned out, he lived near me, so I asked him why I had never seen him before. He said he had gone to private school before now. I would have never hung out with a private school kid before.

We talked all the way home, and I carried his books.

He turned out to be a pretty cool kid. I asked him if he wanted to play football on Saturday with me and my friends. He said yes. We hung out all weekend, and the more I got to know Kyle, the more I liked him. And my friends thought the same of him.

Monday morning came, and there was Kyle with the huge stack of books again.

I stopped him and said, "Damn boy, you are gonna really build some serious muscles with this pile of books everyday!"

He just laughed and handed me half the books.

Over the next four years, Kyle and I became best friends. When we were seniors, we began to think about college. Kyle decided on Georgetown, and I was going to Duke. I knew that we would always be friends, that the miles would never be a problem.

He was going to be a doctor, and I was going for business on a football scholarship. Kyle was valedictorian of his class. I teased him all the time about being a nerd. He had to prepare a speech for graduation. I was so glad it wasn't me having to get up there and speak.

Graduation day, I saw Kyle. He looked great. He was one of those guys that really found himself during high school. He filled out and actually looked good in glasses. He had more dates than me and all the girls loved him! Boy, sometimes I was jealous.

Today was one of those days. I could see that he was nervous about his speech. So, I smacked him on the back and said, "Hey, big guy, you'll be great!"

He looked at me with one of those looks (the really grateful one) and smiled.

"Thanks," he said.

As he started his speech, he cleared his throat, and began. "Graduation is a time to thank those who helped you make it through those tough years. Your parents, your teachers, your siblings, maybe a coach.... but mostly your friends. I am here to tell all of you that being a friend to someone is the best gift you can give them. I am going to tell you a story."

I just looked at my friend with disbelief as he told the story of the first day we met.

He had planned to kill himself over the weekend. He talked of how he had cleaned out his locker so his mom wouldn't have to do it later and was carrying his stuff home.

He looked hard at me and gave me a little smile. "Thankfully, I was saved. My friend saved me from doing the unspeakable."

I heard the gasp go through the crowd as this handsome, popular boy told us all about his weakest moment.

I saw his mom and dad looking at me and smiling that same grateful smile. Not until that moment did I realise its depth.

24.

Build Deeper Relationships by More Fully Appreciating All of the Person

If you took two people whose relationship had broken up and asked them why the relationship hadn't worked out, it's likely both would have a different story. In most cases, particularly if the breakup was acrimonious, each would blame the other.

Obviously both can't be true... or can they?

So often through life, we act as if everything is someone else's fault—as if there is only one objective world. In truth, there is a world for each individual.

> We live in a world of relativity. Everything is relative. This means there are no absolutes... no certainties. Put your hand on a hot stove for a minute, and it seems like an hour. Sit with a pretty girl for an hour, and it seems like a minute. THAT'S relativity.
>
> *Albert Einstein*

Therefore, we have choice. Choice in how we perceive... interpret... and respond.

Having choice means that the difference in good or bad is down to us. It is not inherent in the person, place, or thing—it just depends on how we choose to perceive and relate to the person or thing. Therefore our relationships are really all about us, and where we choose to be in relation to the other person.

A relationship is not about two people trying to be something that they're not in order to fit together. It's not possible to be someone you're not and be happy. Neither can your partner. Sooner or later, you'll get frustrated with your partner, or vice versa.

However, if you are yourself and your partner themselves, you still have choice in how you perceive them and so how you judge them.

Every individual is capable of a full range of emotions. We can all feel happy, sad, frustrated, and ecstatic. Equally, we are all capable of being the full range of behaviours, from angelic to evil.

Some people will come across you and see certain behaviours and emotions and judge you in a certain way. And others will see completely different behaviours and judge you in a completely opposite way. This could even be in response to the same contexts. So one judges you poorly for the same behaviour and demeanour that another judges you highly for. You see, it doesn't matter what you do; however people judge you has far more to do with their history and Operating System than it has to do with your actions.

In the early days of a relationship, the honeymoon stage, couples tend to perceive the behaviours that they rate most highly. Later, in times when you feel a dislike for the person, you will perceive the range that you judge to be more negative. Sometimes, it is even the same behaviour. It is not that they have necessarily changed, but that your displeasure with them—your frustration about something even unrelated to them — has caused you to tune into the negative range of perceptions.

If you want to maintain your relationship and make it more enjoyable, it is possible by remembering what you perceive is a choice.

If you allow frustration and resentments to go unresolved between you, this will create a balloon between you that will grow. This then inclines you towards the negative perceptions.

All frustrations and resentments are, of course, caused by perception. Often in relationships, the Economic Mindset causes us to continually assess if we are generating the maximum return on our investment. Is there a better deal outside for us?

The solution to this is to choose your partner. Rather than looking at your partner to see if he or she matches up, decide to just enjoy them, regardless. Decide to choose them in any context rather than thinking who might be better in a certain area.

Years ago, I asked God to give me a spouse. "You don't own because you didn't ask," God said. Not only did I ask for a spouse, but I also explained what kind of spouse I wanted. I want someone nice, tender, forgiving, passionate, honest, peaceful, generous, understanding, pleasant, warm, intelligent, humorous, attentive, compassionate, and truthful. I even mentioned the physical characteristics I dreamt about.

As time went by, I added the required list of my wanted spouse. One night, in my prayer, God talked to my heart:

"My servant, I cannot give you what you want."

I asked, "Why, God?" and God said, "Because I am God and I am fair. God is the truth, and all I do is true and right."

I asked, "God, I don't understand why I cannot have what I ask from you?"

God answered, "I will explain. It is not fair and right for Me to fulfil your demand because I cannot give something that is not your own self.

It is not fair to give someone who is full of love to you if sometimes you are still hostile; or to give you someone generous if sometimes you can be cruel; or someone forgiving if you still hide revenge; someone sensitive if you are very insensitive..."

He then said to me: "It is better for Me to give you someone who I know could grow to have all qualities you are searching for rather than to make you waste your time finding someone who already has the qualities you want.

Your spouse would then be bone from your bone and flesh from your flesh, and you will see yourself in her, and both of you will be one. Marriage is like a school. It is a life-long span education. It is where you and your partner make adjustment and aim not merely to please each other, but to be better human beings and to make a solid teamwork.

I do not give you a perfect partner, because you are not perfect either. I give you a partner with whom you would grow together."

Source Unknown

❋ *The Sun and Moon appear to move in a similar plane, from due East to due West. Since the Moon is only visible when it is reflecting the light from the Sun, its position will determine how visible it is and the shape that we see. When the Sun and Moon are in the same part of the sky, the Moon will not be visible at all.*

HOW LONG?

A young but earnest Zen student approached his teacher and asked the Zen Master:

"If I work very hard and diligent how long will it take for me to find Zen?"

The Master thought about this, then replied, "Ten years."

The student then said, "But what if I work very, very hard and really apply myself to learn fast — How long then?"

Replied the Master, "Well, twenty years."

"But, if I really, really work at it. How long then?" asked the student.

Source Unknown

"Thirty years," replied the Master.

"But, I do not understand," said the disappointed student. "At each time that I say I will work harder, you say it will take me longer. Why do you say that?"

Replied the Master, "When you have one eye on the goal, you only have one eye on the path."

25.

Relate To Others From Choice, Not Need

I never saw an ugly thing in my life: for let the form of an object be what it may – light, shade, and perspective will always make it beautiful.

John Constable

The ultimate romantic image that many people have of relationships is of them and their partners needing each other and not being able to bear to be apart — each being a different side of the same coin, or a half of something better. Out of the seven billion plus individuals on this planet, they believe one person is the only one… having some unique mystical quality that can complete them. So millions of people go on a quest to find their soul mate, their Mr/Miss Right. The central problem to this basis of need for a relationship is what happens when for one reason or another, the other side cannot fulfil it. You'll begin to feel as if you are lacking or deprived. This frightens you, as you do not feel sufficiently complete alone. Fear turns into frustration at your self-imposed limitations, then to anger, and eventually resentment at being made to feel weak and insecure.

If this cycle happens often enough, it may make you begin to look around for other options to fill your need that is created through your perceived lack.

On the other hand, approaching relationships knowing you are in yourself complete and without need for another to compensate and balance you will change the relationship's basis and so the way you interact.

Now you are not with someone out of the need to be made whole... but simply because you enjoy and prefer being with them.

This removes the pressure of trying to change your partner in order to ensure they supply that which you believe you lack. Since both sides are more relaxed, there is more leeway for each to express him/herself. It's like the difference between a car tyre with no tread and one with a deep tread. There is a reserve, a margin for error, more room for friction—without it seeming to be a matter of life or death for the relationship.

Choosing your partner goes beyond need. Think of the difference in the way that you shop for necessities and luxuries. When you need milk, bread, or sugar, it doesn't really matter if your preferred brand (if you have one) is out of stock. You just take whatever they have because you need it.

Contrast this with shopping for a high-end car, holiday, or designer dress. You won't take just anything; it has to be the one you want, the one that is right for you. You're prepared to wait, look around, be patient, and discriminate in your investment. It's the same difference between choosing and needing a partner or a relationship.

✲ *Both the Moon and Sun travel across the sky in an East-West motion. As the Moon reflects the Sun's light, the brightest side will be towards the direction of the Sun, ie East or West. The line that joins the crescent is at a right angle to this East-West line, giving an approximate North-South line.*

MEMO TO JESUS

TO: Jesus, Son of Joseph

COMPANY: The Woodcrafter's Carpenter Shop, Nazareth

FROM: Jordon Management Consultants, Jerusalem

SUBJECT: Management Report

Thank you for submitting the resumes of the twelve men you have picked for managerial positions in your new organisation.

All of them have now taken our battery of tests, and we have not only run the results through our computers, but also arranged personal interviews for each of them with our psychologist and vocational aptitude consultant.

Source Unknown

219

It is the opinion of the staff that most of your nominees are lacking in background, education, and vocational aptitude for the type of enterprise you are undertaking.

They do not have the team concept. We would recommend that you continue your search for persons of experience in managerial ability and proven capacity.

We have summarised the findings of our study below:

— Simon Peter is emotional, unstable, and given to fits of temper.

— Andrew has absolutely no quality of leadership.

— The two brothers, James and John, the sons of Zebedee, place personal interests above company loyalty.

— Thomas demonstrates a questioning attitude that would tend to undermine morale.

— We believe it is our duty to tell you that Matthew has been blacklisted by the Greater Jerusalem Better Business Bureau.

— James, the son of Alphaeus, and Thaddeus definitely have radical leanings. Additionally, they both registered high scores on the manic-depressive scale.

— However, one of the candidates shows great potential. He's a man of ability and resourcefulness; he is a great networker; has a keen business mind; and has strong contacts in influential circles. He's highly motivated, very ambitious, and adept with financial matters. We recommend Judas Iscariot as your Controller and Chief Operating Officer.

All the other profiles are self-explanatory. We wish you the utmost success in your new venture.

26.

Create Rather Than Compare

The curse of socialisation is the mistaken belief that there is a set standard we should match up to. It causes us to always be looking around and so diffusing attention, rather than focusing on what we can do ourselves.

In relationships, this means that our energies are often diverted from creating our dream relationship to comparing with other relationships. Or comparing other potential relationships.

There is always something else to compare against. You can never be definitively 100% certain that A will be a better bet than B. But if you choose A and keep checking or even jumping from one relationship to another, you'll never invest enough into it to make it as good as it could be.

It's like wanting to invest money. You could spend a lifetime checking out strategies and following tips without ever acting.

Eventually there is a point where if you had just plumped for one method, you would have made more than by procrastinating and prevaricating.

If you are in a relationship and want to continue being in that relationship, forget about what other relationships look like. Your energy and attention will be much better spent on directing it into creating the type of relationship you want to enjoy. There are no rules. You can create a relationship to be however best suits you.

Equally, forget about comparing your partner with other potential partners. If you want to stay in the relationship, focus your attention on the relationship and bring it to life. When you take away the distractions, you are left with much more focus—and so more power. Then you will start to create your perfect relationship.

✻ *The prominent pole star known as the Polaris (or North Star) is aligned with the Earth's axis of rotation. This is a highly visible, but not necessarily the brightest, star in the night sky. The position of the Polaris is less than a degree of the celestial pole, always giving a clear indication of North.*

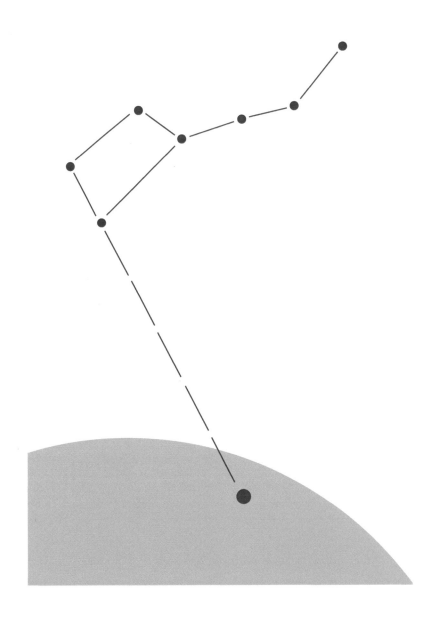

THE SEVEN WONDERS

Junior high school students in Chicago were studying the Seven Wonders of the World. At the end of the lesson, the students were asked to list what they considered to be the Seven Wonders of the World. Though there was some disagreement, the following received the most votes:

1. Egypt's Great Pyramids
2. The Taj Mahal in India
3. The Grand Canyon in Arizona
4. The Panama Canal
5. The Empire State Building
6. St. Peter's Basilica
7. China's Great Wall

Source Unknown

While gathering the votes, the teacher noted that one student, a quiet girl, hadn't turned in her paper yet. So she asked the girl if she was having trouble with her list. The quiet girl replied, "Yes, a little. I couldn't quite make up my mind because there were so many." The teacher said, "Well, tell us what you have, and maybe we can help."

The girl hesitated, then read,
"I think the Seven Wonders of the World are:

1. to touch...
2. to taste...
3. to see...
4. to hear...

(She hesitated a little, and then added...)

5. to feel...
6. to laugh...
7. and to love."

The room was so quiet, you could have heard a pin drop.

27.

Use Differences as a Source of Growth and Improvement

From the conventional romantic perspective of relationships, an argument is a failure. It is a failure because it shows a split, where the aim is for two to be as one, with a shared mind and shared thoughts.

Actually though, differences are the way that you and your relationship are strengthened. We become stronger when we are more inclusive. God, the force of life, or whatever terminology you wish to use, includes everything—the good and the bad; the more we can embrace, the closer to God we become.

The more ideas, facts, people, and situations that remain outside of us, the more potential there is to cause us problems. It is often said that religion has triggered more wars than anything else. The reason for this is because religions often exclude many people. If a religion is based on a chosen people or people needing to adopt a set of beliefs or behaviours to gain access to paradise, then it is a religion based on exclusion— exclusion of non-believers, infidels, or those unworthy according to the rules of the religion.

The purpose of relationships—and everything in life as in relation to you—is to provide a continual source of growth. Eventually the two become one. Not in the sense of sharing the same mind and opinions, but through becoming inclusive enough to embrace and accept the others opinions as an equally valid choice. This then moves us towards the relationship God, Life, or whatever term you wish to use, has with us.

The conventional view assumes that there is only one right way.

So when Mr. Smith thinks A is best and Mrs. Smith thinks B, it appears that one must be right and the other wrong. Therefore, each must argue their case for all they are worth. If they don't then they risk being annihilated, in the sense that their idea—which symbolises them—becomes consumed by the other.

If, however, we allowed the possibility that both could be right—you are then forced to find a more inclusive understanding that embraces both perspectives. This attitude leads to more inclusiveness and so more growth; each partner is more respected and validated, giving them the foundation to explore more deeply and continually grow.

❋ *As the Earth rotates on its axis, the night stars seem to travel around the Earth. The Earth's North Pole is aligned with Polaris' (North Star's) position in the sky. Because of this the North Star appears motionless, providing a constant and dependable point of reference.*

THE MBA AND THE FISHERMAN

The American investment banker was at the pier of a small coastal Mexican village when a small boat with just one fisherman docked.

Inside the small boat were several large yellow fin tuna. The American complimented the Mexican on the quality of his fish and asked how long it took to catch them.

The Mexican replied, "Only a little while."

The American then asked, "Why didn't you stay out longer and catch more fish?"

The Mexican said, "With this, I have more than enough to support my family's needs."

The American then asked, "But what do you do with the rest of your time?"

Source Unknown

The Mexican fisherman said, "I sleep late, fish a little, play with my children, take siesta with my wife, Maria, stroll into the village each evening where I sip wine and play guitar with my amigos. I have a full and busy life."

The American scoffed, "I am a Harvard MBA and could help you. You should spend more time fishing; and with the proceeds, buy a bigger boat: With the proceeds from the bigger boat, you could buy several boats.

Eventually you would have a fleet of fishing boats. Instead of selling your catch to a middleman, you would sell directly to the processor, eventually opening your own cannery.

You would control the product, processing, and distribution. You would need to leave this small coastal fishing village and move to Mexico City, then Los Angeles, and eventually New York, where you will run your ever-expanding enterprise."

The Mexican fisherman asked, "But, how long will this all take?"

To which the American replied, "15 to 20 years."

"But what then?" asked the Mexican.

The American laughed and said that was the best part. "When the time is right, you would announce an IPO and sell your company stock to the public and become very rich—you would make millions."

"Millions?... Then what?"

The American said, "Then you would retire. Move to a small coastal fishing village where you would sleep late, fish a little, play with your kids, take siesta with your wife, stroll to the village in the evenings where you could sip wine and play your guitar with your amigos."

28.

Access Deeper and More Powerful Sources of Motivation

Everything in life has many, many layers and levels to it. And motivation is no different.

No one has ever lacked motivation. Probably the most common area where people talk about motivation is losing weight and exercising.

Now, why is someone overweight?

Because they have too much motivation for the foods that make them put on weight.

Why don't people exercise?

Because they are more motivated to do anything rather than exercise. The problem is not motivation. You are always motivated, but you are motivated for the things that you feel will bring the greatest rewards or the least pain.

Your motivation depends to a great extent on your personality. Introverts are more interested in avoiding pain, whereas extroverts are more concerned with possible rewards. Some people have a longer-term view of life, others care more about now.

So an introvert with a longer-term perspective is far more likely to choose the fat-free option, because he or she wants to avoid the pain of being overweight.

Whereas a more impulsive extrovert will probably go for the chocolate cake, because the reward now is far more exciting than the possible pain in the future.

Everything we think and do comes through the framework of the Economic Mindset. By economic, I don't mean financial, but we do attribute everything with a value. And we continually look to maximise our pleasure and reduce our pain.

So if your motivation drops off, look for what you are valuing more. What are you more motivated towards? The payoff may not be obvious or even now, but on some layer or level, there must be a payoff.

This brings us to another aspect of motivation. Different areas of our lives work on different levels, and as a result access different sources of motivation. The source of motivation you are using will determine how long you stay motivated for.

So for example, we may have a deep-rooted, and so more constant, source of motivation in parenting our children. Yet we may find it a struggle to keep visiting the gym, because our motivation for that issue is much shallower and more swayed by changing circumstances.

There are five levels of motivation that I can think of. And each one has a slightly longer life span than the last. There's:

1. The resolution you make because it's expected of you.

This type of resolution has no real emotional payoff to you. It's just something you are doing because the consequence of not doing it may risk disapproval or standing out and appearing abnormal.

Doing what's expected is easy. It saves you from being nagged and the effort of thinking for yourself. But once you are out of that situation it's hard to maintain, because you have no investment in doing it when you're not being supervised.

2. The resolution you make because you feel bad at the moment.

This type of resolution is made as a kneejerk reaction in the moment to get rid of a pain. So it has an emotional payoff, but as soon as the pain has gone, there is no reason to continue.

It is the motivation to hit out at someone that makes you angry — to seek revenge or to get into a rebound relationship. To seek refuge in chocolate, alcohol, nicotine, or some other feel-good activity.

For example, if you really analyse why people exercise — I used to own a Health Club, so I did — you'll find that they tend to do it because they're fed up with being overweight, or unfit, or whatever. But this isn't a sudden decision. Most have been considering exercising for months, or even years. What really gets them to start is a more intense emotional pain.

Either a doctor scares them into exercising, or more often it's a time when they feel insecure. Perhaps they have just got divorced, or their relationship is hitting a rocky patch and they are thinking of either competing for their partner or being back on the dating market. Whatever the specifics, they feel so bad when they worry that they have to do something to ease the pain. "Yes," they say, "I'm determined to stay on the program this time. I know it's not a quick fix." And they mean it when they say it.

Two or three months later, though, the situation that was causing the pain has resolved itself one way or another. So the incentive for exercising has gone. Yet the grind of going through the boring routine is still there. Sooner or later, the pain of exercising outweighs the relief it used to bring. And then the resolution ends.

3. The resolution you make because you want something.

Sometimes this level comes from wanting something in order to get rid of a pain. And sometimes it just a natural ambition to grow. It lasts until you outgrow the desire or something better comes along.

4. The resolution you make because you want to feel good.

Often people will go through the other level of resolutions. And with each stage of evolution, they find that life in general just starts to feel better after overcoming a problem. Then somewhere, something just clicks, and they realise that they feel better because each problem caused them to grow in order to resolve it. The idea pops into their head that if they were to just grow for the sake of it... life might get more and more enjoyable.

This resolution is deeper and so is based on a far more permanent feeling. Therefore, it lasts for far longer than the previous motivations, which were just passing wants. However, what you want and do to feel good will change as you grow. One time you may want X, but three months or three years (depending on how quickly you are evolving) later, you change your mind about what will make you feel good. Then your resolution will change, possibly before your motivation goes.

5. The resolution you make because it's you.

There are some things that you just feel so strongly about that you absolutely must do them. Equally, there are other actions that are so deeply repulsive to you that you could never do them. This is because they just aren't you. So the motivation for this type of resolution will last for as long as your identity remains constant relative to that action.

You can have different levels of resolutions in different areas of your life. Though, I think, each level of resolution represents a problem or an urge to grow. Overcoming these problems or achieving these desires causes us to grow and evolve. Once we grow, there is no going back. Try not being able to ride a bike or do up your shoelaces. So problems and desires are the stick and the carrot forcing us to evolve.

Eventually, we can reach a stage, where we realise that all along, it was us that created the problems. And if we just accept ourselves and just be ourselves, we can enjoy all of life... and life will then appreciate and enjoy us.

❋ *In the southern hemisphere, the pole is identified by the Southern Cross — not a single bright star as the North Star, but a collection of four. As there is no prominent star close to the celestial pole, it makes finding a clearer indication of South a little more complex.*

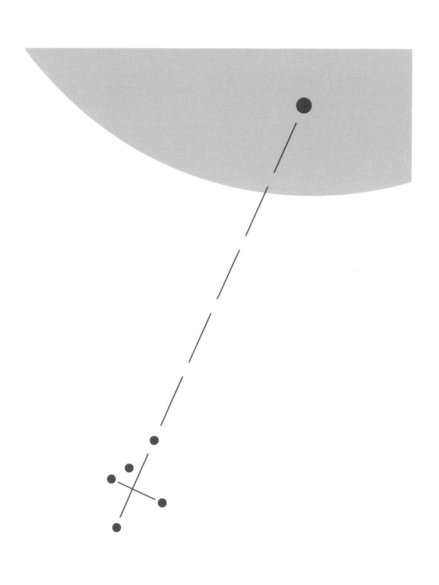

THE GIFT OF LOVE

The passengers on the bus watched sympathetically as the attractive young woman with the white cane made her way carefully up the steps. She paid the driver and, using her hands to feel the location of the seats, walked down the aisle and found the seat he'd told her was empty. Then she settled in, placed her briefcase on her lap, and rested her cane against her leg.

It had been a year since Susan, thirty-four, became blind. Due to a medical misdiagnosis, she had been rendered sightless, and she was suddenly thrown into a world of darkness, anger, frustration, and self-pity.

Once a fiercely independent woman, Susan now felt condemned by this terrible twist of fate to become a powerless, helpless burden on everyone around her. "How could this have happened to me?" she would plead, her heart knotted with anger. But no matter how much she cried or ranted or prayed, she knew the painful truth—her sight was never going to return.

A cloud of depression hung over Susan's once optimistic spirit. Just getting through each day was an exercise in frustration and exhaustion. And all she had to cling to was her husband, Mark.

Mark was an Air Force officer and he loved Susan with all of his heart. When she first lost her sight, he watched her sink into despair and was determined to help his wife gain the strength and confidence she needed to become independent again. Mark's military background had trained him well to deal with sensitive situations, and yet he knew this was the most difficult battle he would ever face.

Finally, Susan felt ready to return to her job, but how would she get there? She used to take the bus, but was now too frightened to get around the city by herself. Mark volunteered to drive her to work each day, even though they worked at opposite ends of the city. At first, this comforted Susan and fulfilled Mark's need to protect his sightless wife who was so insecure about performing the slightest task.

Soon, however, Mark realised that this arrangement wasn't working; it was hectic, and costly. Susan would have to start taking the bus again, he admitted to himself. But just the thought of mentioning it to her made him cringe. She was still so fragile, so angry. How would she react?

Just as Mark predicted, Susan was horrified at the idea of taking the bus again. "I'm blind!" she responded bitterly. "How am I supposed to know where I'm going? I feel like you're abandoning me." Mark's heart broke to hear these words, but he knew what had to be done. He promised Susan that each morning and evening he would ride the bus with her, for as long as it took, until she got the hang of it.

And that is exactly what happened. For two solid weeks, Mark—military uniform and all—accompanied Susan to and from work each day. He taught her how to rely on her other senses, specifically her hearing, to determine where she was and how to adapt to her new environment. He helped her befriend the bus drivers who could watch out for her and save her a seat.

He made her laugh, even on those not-so-good days when she would trip exiting the bus or drop her briefcase. Each morning they made the journey together, and Mark would take a cab back to his office.

Although this routine was even more costly and exhausting than the previous one, Mark knew it was only a matter of time before Susan would be able to ride the bus on her own. He believed in her, in the Susan he used to know before she'd lost her sight, who wasn't afraid of any challenge and who would never, ever quit.

Finally, Susan decided that she was ready to try the trip on her own.

Monday morning arrived, and before she left, she threw her arms around Mark, her temporary bus riding companion, her husband, and her best friend. Her eyes filled with tears of gratitude for his loyalty, his patience, his love. She said good-bye, and for the first time, they went their separate ways.

Monday, Tuesday, Wednesday, Thursday… Each day on her own went perfectly, and Susan had never felt better. She was doing it! She was going to work all by herself!

On Friday morning, Susan took the bus to work as usual. As she was paying for her fare to exit the bus, the driver said, "Boy, I sure envy you."

Susan wasn't sure if the driver was speaking to her or not. After all, who on earth would ever envy a blind woman who had struggled just to find the courage to live for the past year?

Curious, she asked the driver, "Why do you say that you envy me?" The driver responded, "It must feel so good to be taken care of and protected like you are."

Susan had no idea what the driver was talking about, and asked again, "What do you mean?"

The driver answered, "You know, every morning for the past week, a fine looking gentleman in a military uniform has been standing across the corner watching you when you get off the bus. He makes sure you cross the street safely and he watches you until you enter your office building. Then he blows you a kiss, gives you a little salute and walks away. You are one lucky lady."

Tears of happiness poured down Susan's cheeks. For although she couldn't physically see him, she had always felt Mark's presence. She was lucky, so lucky, for he had given her a gift more powerful than sight, a gift she didn't need to see to believe — the gift of love that can bring light where there had been darkness.

29.

Direct Your Own Life With These Three Critical Steps

Once you understand the principles that cause your emotional health and the physical reality you see about you, it is possible to extend and direct your power of attention, to create whichever reality you choose. It doesn't matter if the reality you want to create is a successful relationship, business, or a change in society.

As long as it is consistent with your purpose here on this planet, the process is always the same. Anything in life that will successfully translate from an idea into reality needs to go through these three steps.

Firstly, you must understand and use the three key cycles of life: Dream, Dare, and Do.

The three cycles to everything in life are:

1. Dream of what you want.
2. Dare to plan and prepare.
3. Do it.

Generally, people try to jump in at step 3, so they are not clear exactly what they want... or exactly what to do. Because they are muddled and confused, they know something might go wrong—but they're not sure what.

They begin trying to do something with only a vague idea of what they want, but they don't know if they can do it or what might go wrong. And then they wonder why they aren't motivated enough.

People are always advocating writing down your goals. It is not the fact of having written goals that makes you successful; it is the clarity you have of what you want to create.

People generally fall into three broad groups:

1. Those who have forgotten what excites them. So now they may have difficulty in dreaming. They have their foot pressed so hard on the brake that they cannot even move.
2. Those who have a dream, but are too afraid to act on it. These are scared to move, so they don't push the accelerator.
3. Those who have difficulty in bringing their dream to fruition. This group can move, but they can't steer in the direction they want to go in.

All of the problems essentially boil down to a lack of clarity. Once you have the clarity to see your dream as if it were already here, the steps to create it will be so clear that it will be like copying from a template.

It took our earliest ancestors centuries to invent fire and tools. Yet if you or I were transported back into their time, we would immediately think of using these to make life easier, only because these have become so real and obvious to us. This is what dreaming does for you. The longer you dream, the clearer the creation seems. Therefore it needs less courage to implement it.

If you pay less attention to your dream than to reality, you will need a great deal of courage, because it then only seems like a pipe dream. But when you have spent hours examining the idea from your imagination, you become as familiar with the dream object as reality. And so the question of it not existing becomes ridiculous.

This is the plasticity of human experience. Things are real only if you pay them enough attention to make them so. People say, "But it's not real, is it? I can't hold it in my hand."

No, but can you hold your worries and anxieties in your hand? Yet you still pay attention to them.

The butterflies you get in your stomach before making a speech... are they real?

The feeling of love when you see your partner or child, is that real?

Reality is only what you believe to be real. If you focus your attention on your dreams, in time it will seem real. At that point, you can deconstruct the way it was created and follow those steps to bring it into reality. Without that level of attention, though, you will lack the courage, belief, ability, and knowledge to bring it into reality.

Dream until it is so clear that you know exactly what steps to take. Dream until you are so excited that you cannot procrastinate; you must make it come true.

Then is the natural time to move into the Dare stage. Many people know exactly what to do, but don't do it—sometimes for lack of motivation, and other times because they are afraid. This is why the Dare stage is so important. This is the planning of how to make it happen.

Many people fall at this hurdle. They get scared and doubt themselves. Instead of following their dream, they chase the easiest way—or the least risk, or most money. This is where people begin to justify "a means to an end".

And before you know it, you have sold out your vision and integrity for something as temporary as money or status. You get the money or the status... but can't understand why it doesn't feel as good, as you expected it to. The result is millions of us settling for a lower quality life and relationship than they dream of—and never being recognised for what they could do.

It will be natural for you to lose sight of your dream... to dilute it... or to get too afraid to continue with it. In these times, just ease up on yourself; don't try to force it through. If you force it, you'll kill your enthusiasm and end up selling out your dream for a compromise that ultimately destroys your dream. Instead, slip back into the dream stage. We too often think that everything has to move forward at a great speed. Sometimes it is natural to slip back, regain your purpose, motivation, and enthusiasm. Then the next step will soon become clear again.

The final stage is the cycle of actually doing it. In most things in life, we don't jump straight in and do it perfectly first time. We need practice. In anything worth doing, we need to find our own route. We need to make a few mistakes and go up some dead ends to understand what is going to work, what isn't, and why. After doing this for a while, we create a map of knowledge, just like we create a map of our neighbourhood

When you first moved to your home, didn't you make a few wrong turns? Eventually all those wrong turns create a map in your head. So now when someone asks you directions, you can quickly find the best way to get there. Likewise, you can be become just as confident in living out your dream.

But because most people jump in at this cycle without dreaming and daring, they are already lacking motivation and courage. In their mind, perhaps they already say to themselves:

"I'll just try this out."

They dip their toe in the water… And if their unconvincing attempt results in anything less than overwhelming success, they decide it won't work.

"Oh, well, I gave it a shot," they'll say.

Then they will find a hundred and one reasons to explain why "IT" wouldn't and couldn't work for them.

Wrong.

You see, life is so simple, if only you fit in with it. Everything has a natural cycle to it. You wouldn't try to bake a cake, without putting the ingredients in first, but so many people try to create a better life without knowing what the ingredients are… or even what recipe they are using.

Some people have a problem with this concept, as they believe that this is interfering with God's plans. However, if it is not through you, me, and everyone else, how is God's wonder and splendour ever going to manifest on earth?

We are the vessels, the pipelines, for God's force. If it makes it easier for you to accept, think about it this way:

God has created a swimming pool (the world). Just an empty hole isn't much use, so he needs to fill it up with water. So he uses a hose (us) to fill the pool. We can direct the water where we want. We can fill the deep end (be wealthy) first or the shallow end (lack).

He doesn't care which; he knows the water will settle down, find its own place, and move about. So the force is his, but you get to choose where it is directed.

It's difficult to grasp this point. It goes against everything you have ever known. This is why people have difficulty with it. The world teaches that you take what you have, and then make the best you can from it.

Wrong. So wrong.

This is why people have no motivation to lose weight, to go to work, and so on.

The event is created by the thought. You think, then do. You think, then attract.

It is your dream, your vision, that determines the level of energy, enthusiasm, and ability you will access for your project. You know how with something you are interested in, work is not a chore—because you understand the value of what you are doing. You know how important it is for you.

When you get such a dream that you truly believe will change the world—that is when you have the ability, the energy, and anything else you need to make it happen.

> Dream lofty dreams, and as you dream so shall you become. Your vision is the promise of what you shall one day be; your Ideal is the prophecy of what you shall at last unveil.
>
> The greatest achievement was at first and for a time a dream.
>
> The oak sleeps in the acorn; the bird waits in the egg; and in the highest vision of the soul a waking angel stirs.
>
> Your circumstances may be uncongenial, but they shall not long remain so when you perceive an Ideal and strive to reach it.

James Allen

It is only the clarity of vision that separates Gandhi, Mother Theresa, and Martin Luther King, Jr., from people who everyday go to work and struggle to maintain enthusiasm and energy throughout their day. There are many other people brighter, richer, younger, and fitter that cannot do as much because they do not call the energy and inspiration through them for mighty results.

If you do not have enough—of anything: money, time, fun, whatever—it is because you have not asked for enough. It is not that you are being greedy to ask for more. It is that you expect so little of God to ask for so little.

When you have a use for millions of pounds, for hours of free time to spend as you wish, for tons of fun, for joy, for excitement, for passion, love, and everything else you want; when that purpose is so clear, so exciting, so tantalising that you can taste it— then you'll find the money, the time, and so on.

What most people do is what we have all been taught to do.

Instead of digging an empty hole to create our swimming pool, we find a puddle. It's not our own, but we pass it, and because we are scared that this huge, infinite universe will not have anywhere better to stay than this tiny muddy puddle, we set up home here.

This puddle doesn't really suit us... but it's home now, and it's better than the dry patches outside. At least there is some water.

Occasionally there will be a little rain, or a trickle from the pool further along the path. But when we look at where we live, we'll see what we have done and think *I can't do that*. And we can't, but only because we have not found and prepared our own hole... and then connected ourselves to the water tap.

Your imagination is the catalogue of possibilities. You may order whatever you like. But it will give you nothing more than what you have ordered. Be sure that you want it. Often people will say I want X. Really, though, what they want is a new experience to grow. At the same time, they are fearful that any change may rob them of things they hold dearly. So they pull the thing they want and then push it away at the same time.

Then what you have done with your thoughts is you have found yourself a swimming pool (remember the hose analogy)

—your niche in life. Now keep the force flowing, amplify it, and you will fill your pool with all you need.

So your dream creates a hole, which expands the world by adding something that doesn't yet exist or fills a gap. The bigger the hole, the more of life's force will flow through you.

People like Mother Theresa and Nelson Mandela achieved great things not because they were great—but because their need was great. Need is only a perception. If you empathise so strongly with a group or situation that you feel must be changed, so greatly that you are willing to step up and solve the problem, then your perceived need is far greater than if you were to live what you might call a more everyday routine.

This applies to all fields. If you dream for so long that you truly believe you are going to be a world-famous star, billionaire businessman, life-changing visionary, or whatever, your perceived need will be far greater. And so you'll pull through more life force, which brings through the talents and energy to bring your dream into reality.

It's important that your dream focuses beyond something like money or fame. These won't create enough pull.

What is it that you want the money, the fame, or the power for?

Many people wish to have more money. Sometimes they even get around to writing down their goals. They may set down a goal for a million pounds. Yet in their dream they are only clearing their £20,000 debts, spending £10,000 on a holiday, and have a vague idea of being wealthy.

Firstly, this doesn't make you believe it. Even to you, it only feels like a pipe dream. So you can't deconstruct the steps to take.

Secondly, this dream of you feeling more comfortable is the spiritual equivalent of a pain killer. It's about eliminating a pain rather than the alchemy of transforming the discomfort into growth and expansion. In no way does it expand the universe. And that is the point of life: expansion and evolution.

Thirdly, it's based on a mistake. Money and all the other symbols are just the tools of life. They are a human construct that makes us more efficient. Money is not your ultimate goal. When people say that they want money, they really want one of two things.

One is that they want freedom from restriction of watching what they spend, the hassle of being in debt, or a feeling of security.

The other is that they want it for something specific. So stop asking the universe to deliver in used ten-pound notes by Friday and just start asking for what you want. Then it may turn up in the money to buy it, or it may turn up in another way. It doesn't matter.

It's all the same thing.

Maintaining your dream directs your life force that flows through, wherever your attention is focused. This in time, if held consistently, will fill the hole you've created. Usually by the time that we've set on something and started to get the wheels in motion, we switch our attention elsewhere. It's like a car going in one direction and then reversing — over and over again. You never end up getting anywhere.

Once you've set this process in motion, it's important not to set your definitions so tightly that you'll only recognise it, if it turns up in the exact form you expected. Say, for example, you want more money. With our limited understanding of the universe, you may think this means a check in the post. However it may turn up in a work bonus, a business opportunity, or even unexpected presents. We have such a limited understanding of the world that we can't imagine the form it will come in without upsetting the balance of everyone else's reality. The universe matches our intentions up with those of all the people around us that we don't even know, and then creates the perfect situation to give to each what they have asked for.

You can't micromanage the whole process. If you try, you'll lose your connection and cut off the life force that flows through you. But if you give up control, you'll get to direct where to aim the flow.

Then pay attention to even the smallest sign, such as even finding some coins down the back of the sofa. With your attention and appreciation, these will grow in magnitude.

Focus only on the thing that you want—not what has happened, could happen, or that you wished would happen—just what is in front of you at the moment. With every shift of your attention, you are starving the thing you previously wanted to create of the life force it needs to manifest.

Then, in the time that is right for you, life will deliver.

In the meantime, how can you be sure it's on its way?

How do you feel?

There are two states you can be in about something you want.

The Tantrum State

Of course, we become more refined and we rationalise our justifications in more sophisticated ways. Essentially, though, our emotional state is the same as that of a two-year-old in a temper tantrum.

Our focus is on what is blocking us from having what we want. This makes us feel bad. After a while, as we focus more attention on what blocks us, we will have more detailed and sophisticated explanations. In time, we'll believe these more strongly and so get further away from the thing we want. Maybe we'll even shut off from wanting things and feel numb, depressed, lifeless, and stagnant.

The Creation State

The second state is where you are on the path to what you want. Think of it this way: you dig a hole in the ground, through your thoughts, for what you want.

What you want is in a bowl that would fit perfectly into the hole you have dug. But at the moment, there are obstacles blocking you from having what you want. These are like sticks holding the bowl (what you want) apart from your hole.

Often there are many obstacles between you and what you want.

So you have many bowls separated from each other by sticks propping them up.

So the process is to identify what the first obstacle is between you and the thing you want. Tackle it and knock the stick away. The bowl will fall into the ground.

Repeat this over and over, and sooner or later, the thing you want will fall into the hole you dug, and you will have created that which you wanted.

Some say to this, "But it seems like such an effort."

Perhaps.

The key point is this: as you are tackling the obstacles and focusing on what you want, you feel good. You feel excitement, passion, and life flowing through your veins.

It isn't really even about the end goal. It's about the journey. And you can know you are travelling towards what you want if you feel good and away from it if you feel bad.

☀ *As the Earth orbits the Sun through the year's cycle, the Sun appears to move on the celestial sphere against the background of the fixed stars. The curving path of the Sun is called the ecliptic, which passes through a series of twelve constellations, the Zodiac.*

LET IT BE

Once Buddha was walking from one town to another town with a few of his followers. This was in the initial days. While they were travelling, they happened to pass a lake. They stopped there and Buddha told one of his disciples, "I am thirsty. Do get me some water from that lake there."

The disciple walked up to the lake. When he reached it, he noticed that some people were washing clothes in the water and, right at that moment, a bullock cart started crossing through the lake. As a result, the water became very muddy, very turbid. The disciple thought, "How can I give this muddy water to Buddha to drink!" So he came back and told Buddha, "The water in there is very muddy. I don't think it is fit to drink."

Source Unknown

After about half an hour, again Buddha asked the same disciple to go back to the lake and get him some water to drink. The disciple obediently went back to the lake. This time he found that the lake had absolutely clear water in it. The mud had settled down and the water above it looked fit to be had. So he collected some water in a pot and brought it to Buddha.

Buddha looked at the water, and then he looked up at the disciple and said, "See what you did to make the water clean. You let it be …and the mud settled down on its own — and you got clear water.… Your mind is also like that. When it is disturbed, just let it be. Give it a little time. It will settle down on its own. You don't have to put in any effort to calm it down. It will happen. It is effortless."

What did Buddha emphasise here? He said, "It is effortless." Having 'peace of mind' is not a strenuous job; it is an effortless process. When there is peace inside you, that peace permeates to the outside. It spreads around you and in the environment, such that people around start feeling that peace and grace.

30.
Go Beyond Fear

Ultimately the only thing in life that stops us from living the life of our dreams is ourselves.

We limit the amount of life force that flows through us through our openness to life and its experiences. We choose our beliefs. Most of our beliefs are handed down from generation to generation and accepted without question, just because everyone agrees that's the way it's always been. We just get trained into believing certain things and stuff them into a dark cupboard in the recesses of our mind and never consider them again. Yet these beliefs determine the reality that we see.

Change your beliefs and you change the entire landscape of your world. Our beliefs create a structure — our Operating System. As the force of life flows through our beliefs and so determines what we think, say and do, this creates the world we see about us.

Different beliefs would lead us to think, speak, or act differently. This would evoke a different reaction from the people around us or even cause us to be in a different place with different people around us. We'd get a different experience of life and so feel different emotions.

Of course, at times for everyone, life has its tough moments. Equally we all have many, many opportunities, but so many people just don't see them.

The major reason that we don't see them, or act on those we see, is fear. So many people feel anxious walking into a room with other people in it, or trying out something new. Almost everything in life is inhibited, limited, or ruined to some extent by fear.

It's fear that stops us from sharing our true self and our talents with the world.

It's fear that stops us from enjoying relationships as intimate and honest as they could be.

It's fear that blocks millions of people from doing anything more exciting than sitting in front of the telly, night after night.

It's fear that makes us settle for the certainty of ordinary, rather than the excitement of the incredible.

Yet again, it only ruins our lives because we misunderstand the role fear plays in our lives.

Fear comes about from uncertainty. Physical fear is a protection against danger. If a hungry lion were creeping up behind you, wouldn't you want some kind of warning? Fear is like the warning light in your car that tells you you're low on oil.

Emotional fear serves a similar purpose. When you begin to dream and you feel fear, it is caused by the friction of the life force flowing through your beliefs. The fear comes from the conflict between the dream and a belief in opposition to your dream.

The greater your fear, the more life force flowing through you, and so the more power and importance connected to the dream. Once you identify the opposing belief and change it, your fear will transform into a momentum that will speed up the process of bringing your dream to life.

Usually, though, we misunderstand this—and the fear becomes so great that it paralyses us. Instead of taking this as encouragement—that our dream is on its way—we try to dull down the fear. The side effect of this is to dilute or ignore our dreams. Instead we settle for that which doesn't cause such uncomfortable feelings. The other side of this is that it bores us and makes us feel less than we know we could be.

Many people think that beliefs are set in stone. This isn't true. Everything you believe, you believe for a reason. Most of the time it was a choice we made many years ago and now we'd choose differently. However, as life is so fast paced, we've never gotten around to reviewing our beliefs. Getting clearer about what exactly is frightening you will bring you to the obstructing belief.

Then, if you analyse and examine the information on which the belief is based, you will sooner or later find something that isn't true. When you fill in the gaps in your knowledge, you can choose to base your belief on the new evidence. And as the life force flows through your new beliefs... your dream will now begin to take shape.

PRAYING HANDS

Back in the fifteenth century, in a tiny village near Nuremberg, lived a family with eighteen children. Eighteen!

In order merely to keep food on the table for this mob, the father and head of the household, a goldsmith by profession, worked almost eighteen hours a day at his trade and any other paying chore he could find in the neighbourhood

Despite their seemingly hopeless condition, two of the children had a dream. They both wanted to pursue their talent for art, but they knew full well that their father would never be financially able to send either of them to Nuremberg to study at the Academy.

After many long discussions at night in their crowded bed, the two boys finally worked out a pact. They would toss a coin. The loser

Source Unknown

265

would go down into the nearby mines and, with his earnings, support his brother while he attended the academy.

Then, when that brother who won the toss completed his studies, in four years, he would support the other brother at the academy, either with sales of his artwork or, if necessary, also by labouring in the mines.

They tossed a coin on a Sunday morning after church. Albrecht Durer won the toss and went off to Nuremberg.

Albert went down into the dangerous mines and, for the next four years, financed his brother, whose work at the academy was almost an immediate sensation. Albrecht's etchings, his woodcuts, and his oils were far better than those of most of his professors, and by the time he graduated, he was beginning to earn considerable fees for his commissioned works.

When the young artist returned to his village, the Durer family held a festive dinner on their lawn to celebrate Albrecht's triumphant homecoming. After a long and memorable meal, punctuated with music and laughter, Albrecht rose from his honoured position at the head of the table to drink a toast to his beloved brother for the years of sacrifice that had enabled Albrecht to fulfil his ambition.

His closing words were, "And now, Albert, blessed brother of mine, it is your turn. Now you can go to Nuremberg to pursue your dream, and I will take care of you."

All heads turned in eager expectation to the far end of the table where Albert sat, tears streaming down his pale face, shaking his lowered head from side to side while he sobbed and repeated, over and over, "No... no, no, no."

Finally, Albert rose and wiped the tears from his cheeks. He glanced down the long table at the faces he loved, and then, holding his hands close to his right cheek, he said softly, "No, brother. I cannot go to Nuremberg. It is too late for me. Look... look what four years in the mines have done to my hands! The bones in every finger have been smashed at least once, and lately I have been suffering from arthritis so badly in my right hand that I cannot even hold a glass to return your toast, much less make delicate lines on parchment or canvas with a pen or a brush. No, brother... for me it is too late."

More than 450 years have passed. By now, Albrecht Durer's hundreds of masterful portraits, pen and silver-point sketches, watercolours, charcoals, woodcuts, and copper engravings hang in every great museum in the world, but the odds are great that you, like most people, are familiar with only one of Albrecht Durer's works. More than merely being familiar with it, you very well may have a reproduction hanging in your home or office.

One day, to pay homage to Albert for all that he had sacrificed, Albrecht Durer painstakingly drew his brother's abused hands with palms together and thin fingers stretched skyward.

He called his powerful drawing simply, "Hands," but the entire world almost immediately opened their hearts to his great masterpiece and renamed his tribute of love, "The Praying Hands."

The next time you see a copy of that touching creation, take a second look. Let it be your reminder, if you still need one, that no one — no one — ever makes it alone!

31.
Stand on the Shoulders of Giants

Everything in life is made from the same four building blocks: hydrogen, carbon, oxygen, and nitrogen. So everything you ever see, however different and unique it may seem, has in its structure the same building blocks. In the same way, every new idea, technique, or mental tool is just a different combination of the same building blocks.

When you read a book or take a course, essentially what you are getting is the fruit from a tree. They have taken a number of seed ideas, planted them, nurtured them, and watched them grow into strong trees. Year after year, these trees will produce fruit.

Now the fruit on its own, looks nice when it's fresh, and tastes great. But two weeks later, it's rotten; it doesn't look so great and it tastes awful. This is just like the way that many people learn something from a book or course; they feel confident in it, but they do not have the mental infrastructure to nourish and maintain the idea.

So they'll come across a situation and they'll think, "Hmm, I learnt how to deal with this... now let me think — I need to do X and then Y, and what was that other thing...?"

Now perhaps if you are able to devote the time, you can integrate the concepts into a mental infrastructure that supports and allows the concepts to develop. But it is only by becoming the idea that you fully understand it. You do not get this from others, or books, or courses. They will give you seeds, but you must grow and nourish them.

The key is to take the main idea from a book or course — not to use the idea as a substitute for your own thoughts. Process the ideas down to their root and mix them altogether for your own unique life philosophy. My intention in this book has been to give you a number of fairly common flaws in our cultural operating system, so that you can examine if they are really true for you, and if not, change them.

It isn't necessary to reinvent every idea. We are here at this time and era in history not to start again in every generation, but to build upon the past. So our job is to discard, refine, and synthesise concepts and ideas.

I can't understand why people are frightened of new ideas. I'm frightened of the old ones.

John Cage

Although we do not need to reinvent the wheel, we do need to update and refine the ideas we currently hold. Tradition is not a valid reason for believing something. Businesses have learned that if they don't identify the loopholes and weaknesses in their products and strategies, they will be overtaken by their competitors. They call it Creative Destruction. It's not a new concept. It happened to the dinosaurs. It doesn't matter how big or powerful you are; if you don't change, when the tide changes you're going to get swept away.

Now, through this book, you have been given concepts, processes, and ideas. In themselves, they are as worthless as the greatest speech delivered without a listener. But planted, nourished, and developed, they are all you need to make everything you could wish for in your lifetime.

It's down to you now.

How many creative ways can you apply them in your life?

Which will you discard?

How will you refine them?

What new combinations will you make of them?

I'd love to hear from you, how these ideas have affected your life.

Let me know at *rob@firstfacenorth.com*

THE TRIPLE FILTER TEST

In ancient Greece, Socrates was reputed to hold knowledge in high esteem. One day, an acquaintance met the great philosopher and said, "Do you know what I just heard about your friend?"

"Hold on a minute," Socrates replied. "Before telling me anything, I'd like you to pass a little test. It's called the Triple Filter Test."

"Triple filter?"

"That's right," Socrates continued. "Before you talk to me about my friend, it might be a good idea to take a moment and filter what you're going to say. That's why I call it the triple filter test. The first filter is truth. Have you made absolutely sure that what you are about to tell me is true?"

"No," the man said, "Actually I just heard about it and…"

Source Unknown

"All right," said Socrates. "So you don't really know if it's true or not. Now, let's try the second filter, the filter of Goodness. Is what you are about to tell me about my friend something good?"

"No, on the contrary…"

"So," Socrates continued, "you want to tell me something bad about him, but you're not certain it's true. You may still pass the test though, because there's one filter left: the filter of Usefulness. Is what you want to tell me about my friend going to be useful to me?"

"No, not really…"

"Well," concluded Socrates, "if what you want to tell me is neither true nor good nor even useful, why tell it to me at all?"

32.

Know That You Deserve It.
All Of It.

When people used to ask what my website was about, I used to say Happiness, feeling somewhat stupid. And they'd laugh. I felt stupid, because I knew happiness meant something different to them than it did to me.

They understood happiness to be something frivolous, something to worry about after the important concerns were taken care of. To them happiness was the momentary elation when something really pleasant happens — maybe like eating chocolate, or how you feel after a relaxing massage.

To me, though, happiness is the purpose and the scorecard of life. Happiness is the pure experience of life. It is the state where you live exactly as you are supposed to — not by adhering to laws and etiquettes, but by living in accordance with your natural design. Less inhibition and anxiety and more authenticity.

You see, when you live in such a way, your mind is completely focused on whatever you pay attention to. As a result, you have 100% of your intelligence, creativity, resilience, and energy available to apply towards whatever goals you are pursuing

—much as a computer without lots of applications open can run faster and more efficiently.

In contrast, when you are stressed or upset, your mind keeps drifting back to whatever is bothering you, literally eating away at your mental resources. Therefore, you may only be able to access 60% of your cognitive resources to the task in hand.

Even beyond this, being happy makes the world a different place. It's like the difference in outlook and perspective between a bright, sunny day with clear blue sky and a wet miserable day.

Life is just so simple. It's like breathing. But we've all grown up in an environment which has taught us we have to follow more rules than we know in order to deserve anything. Then maybe if we've been a good boy or girl, we'll be given stuff that will make us happy—just like our early teachers gave us a gold star.

You can have anything that you want. You don't have to jump through any hoops to get it. The world will give you any experience, any feeling, or anything that you want. It's you that pushes it away.

Why?

Because you don't believe you deserve it—either because you feel you need to qualify for it, or because you don't believe you are a worthy enough person.

People get what they believe they deserve, not what they actually deserve. There is no universal judge, or supreme court, sitting in judgement. Everything is available to you, however good or bad you are. Look around and you'll find people who have everything, yet you consider them to be undeserving. And equally, you'll find those whom you see as deserving with nothing.

This applies to everything in life. Relationships, success, happiness, fun. Let's take money as an example. It's not about hard work. Life doesn't care about any of that stuff. It wouldn't matter if you worked flat-out a hundred hours a week of the hardest labour for twenty years—still all your earnings wouldn't dent Bill Gates's.

Neither is it intelligence. Many of the smartest people in the world earn meagre wages.

Nor is it skill. You can be the greatest tiddlywinks player in the whole world; still you are unlikely to earn fortunes.

It all comes down to believing that you deserve it. And so people who feel undeserving or don't believe that the world will deliver for them unconsciously put the brakes on. This then translates into missing opportunities, or action that is less effective and less productive, than it could have been. Then they get what they believed they deserve.

In much the same way, you'll see examples of people who win fortunes without raising a finger. Or you'll hear stories of some film or pop star's outrageous demands. They make these—and get them—because they feel so deserving in that specific area.

That doesn't mean that being deserving means acting like a spoilt brat. That's just how some people get themselves to feel deserving.

And because you feel deserving in one area of your life, that doesn't necessarily mean you will feel deserving in other areas.

Often great wealth can cause a lack of happiness in relationships. It doesn't have to, but the person concerned may believe it does and so unconsciously creates those situations. Maybe because they believe people value them for their money or because they expect money to solve problems that it can't.

It is feeling deserving that opens you up to the ideas, abilities, and opportunities that bring to you whatever it is you want. All the wisdom, skill, and circumstances are available to you. You only have to tune into what you want by allowing yourself to receive and act on inspiration.

Much of the pain that we feel comes not from what happens, but from the endless replays and brooding on what happens—the resentment, anger, and frustration from trying to appeal to what is fair or justified. Almost every day there is a story in the newspaper of someone who is by most accounts morally justified in their actions. yet through a legal technicality, they end up punished. In the same way, life doesn't work on your version of what actions are fair or justified. It just is.

We often look at life and think the things we want are rewards.

The universe understands that things, relationships, and experiences are just the tools we use for evolution. So as the force of life flows through us, we experience desire and repulsion.

These work to get us to move through life, to experience more.

Say, for example, you have a driving ambition to start your own business. Ultimately, at the deepest levels of your being, it isn't for money or success or even more time. You are experiencing that desire in order to put yourself into situations that will bring you more growth.

In the same way, repulsion at your current work may be to get you into a new job to experience something new because the new is what you need to grow and evolve you.

BUZZ AND THE QUIET KIWI

By good fortune, I was able to raft down the Motu River in New Zealand twice during the last year. The magnificent four-day journey traverses one of the last wilderness areas in the North Island.

The first expedition was led by "Buzz", an American guide with a great deal of rafting experience and many stories to tell of mighty rivers such as the Colorado. With a leader like Buzz, there was no reason to fear any of the great rapids on the Motu.

The first half day in the gentle upper reaches was spent developing teamwork and co-ordination. Strokes had to be mastered, and the discipline of following commands without question was essential. In the boiling fury of a rapid, there would be no room for any mistake. When Buzz bellowed above the roar of the water, an instant reaction was essential.

Source Unknown

We mastered the Motu. In every rapid, we fought against the river and we overcame it. The screamed commands of Buzz were matched only by the fury of our paddles, as we took the raft exactly where Buzz wanted it to go.

At the end of the journey, there was a great feeling of triumph. We had won. We proved that we were superior. We knew that we could do it. We felt powerful and good. The mystery and majesty of the Motu had been overcome.

The second time I went down the Motu, the experience I had gained should have been invaluable, but the guide on this journey was a very softly spoken Kiwi. It seemed that it would not even be possible to hear his voice above the noise of the rapids.

As we approached the first rapid, he never even raised his voice. He did not attempt to take command of us or the river. Gently and quietly he felt the mood of the river and watched every little whirlpool. There was no drama and no shouting. There was no contest to be won. He loved the river.

We sped through each rapid with grace and beauty and, after a day, the river had become our friend, not our enemy. The quiet Kiwi was not our leader, but only the person whose sensitivity was more developed than our own. Laughter replaced the tension of achievement.

Soon the quiet Kiwi was able to lean back and let all of us take turns as leader. A quiet nod was enough to draw attention to the things our lack of experience prevented us from seeing. If we made a mistake, then we laughed, and it was the next person's turn.

We began to penetrate the mystery of the Motu. Now, like the quiet Kiwi, we listened to the river and we looked carefully for all those things we had not even noticed the first time.

At the end of the journey, we had overcome nothing except ourselves. We did not want to leave behind our friend, the river. There was no contest, and so nothing had been won. Rather we had become one with the river.

It remains difficult to believe that the external circumstances of the two journeys were similar. The difference was in an attitude and a frame of mind. At the end of the journey, it seemed that there could be no other way. Given the opportunity to choose a leader, everyone would have chosen someone like Buzz. At the end of the second journey, we had glimpsed a very different vision and we felt humble —and intensely happy.

33.

Have It All, but Not All
On the Same Plate

I promised earlier that I would explain how you can have everything you ever want. Here's time to deliver.

Imagine that every single thing you want is represented by a colour. Success may be blue, happiness yellow, calmness green, and so on.

Now when you say, "I want success," this request is so vague and broad that when you choose, that the whole screen becomes blue.

Soon you miss happiness and say, "I just want to be happy." Now the screen turns yellow. At first you say, "Ah, this is what I missed."

But soon again you feel deprived. And you say, "I want success and happiness." Now you get a blend of the two.

Do you get the picture? When you make broad, unspecific requests, you get broad, unspecific results. And so what you choose now blocks out what you chose previously.

So how do you get everything?

You paint a picture with your thoughts. Like an artist, you set out where you want each colour. You say, "I want success, but I want it here, here, and here—this shade, and just like this.

Then I also want calmness, and it will look like this." And with each thought, you transfer every want that you have into a big picture—your vision and overview of how you want your life to look.

And once your vision is clear to you, your action to bring this vision to life is no more difficult than painting by numbers. But without the vision, you do not know if you will like what you are painting until you see it. Then you have to rub it out—or worse yet, scrunch up the paper and start all over again. Then it all seems such a struggle, impossible even. After rubbing out numerous mistakes and starting with a clean sheet a few times, most people give up and learn to live with the blotches and smears they don't like. They say, "This is life. It wasn't ever meant to be perfect."

But now you know it can be—if you really want it to be...

☀ *There are 365 revolutions of the Earth during the time it takes to complete its orbital journey around the Sun. The orbit is elliptical with a variance of approximately 53 million miles.*

When one door of happiness closes, another opens; but often we look so long at the closed door that we do not see the one which has opened for us.

— HELEN KELLER

Remember that happiness is a way of travel—not a destination.

— ROY M GOODMAN

Happiness is essentially a state of going somewhere, wholeheartedly, one-directionally, without regret or reservation.

— WILLIAM H SHELDON

LEARN TO LOVE THEM

A man who took great pride in his lawn found himself with a large crop of dandelions. He tried every method he knew to get rid of them. Still they plagued him.

Finally he wrote to the Department of Agriculture.

He enumerated all the things he had tried and closed his letter with the question: "What shall I do now?"

In due course, the reply came: "We suggest you learn to love them."

Source Unknown

34.
Be Free

We live in the era of the thirty-second sound bite. None of us have time to go too deeply into very much, and so style often counts for more than substance.

The problem is that we often misunderstand or misinterpret the sound bite, because we do not have all the information that supports the conclusion. The conclusion is like a tabletop. Without knowing the assumptions, which support it as the legs support a table, you won't get the full meaning.

The full meaning allows you to use the belief. You can use, adapt, or discard it to best serve you... rather than being trapped. And ultimately, beliefs are just tools. None are inherently any truer than another. They depend on the perspective we look from and where we are at this moment in time.

So in the chapters up to now, I have given you as much information and perspectives as I can, without personally speaking to you, to support this conclusion.

Happiness is...

Freedom.

That's really all happiness is about. Think about it. What makes you unhappy?

Analyse it down to its root and you'll discover in some way it is about feeling trapped.

- Sometimes it's feeling trapped by a lack of money.
- Sometimes it's feeling trapped in a relationship.
- Or trapped in behaving a certain way for fear of the reaction of others.
- Trapped in a job.
- Stuck in a situation.

In a million different ways, we bind ourselves up in the rules. We get hung up on a set way for things to be done and then make ourselves miserable.

We are only bound and trapped in our thoughts. Change your thoughts, be open to new possibilities... then freedom and happiness are yours.

Every unhappiness is created only by ourselves. And the thing that perpetuates that unhappiness is our attempts at justifying and rationalising our unhappiness.

BE
OPEN...

BE
FREE...

BE
YOU...

BE HAPPY.

✳ *Our understanding and observation of the universe around us can empower self-orientation. Whether the landscape we are traversing is physical or emotional, navigation is made simpler by our ability to appreciate the journey.*

Our measurement of our universe encompasses all matter, and all matter is a measure of time and space. Being able to read this relationship helps us to better understand our own course.

Acknowledgements

I don't think people generally recognise, or appreciate, just how important other people are in influencing and shaping our lives. The kid who picked on you in primary school, the teacher that inspired you, the girl/boy who rejected you, the coach who picked or dumped you from a team — all of them may have seemed to have had only a cameo role, yet they are all pivot points that lead you to becoming who and what you are now.

And so I have many people to thank, who have shaped and influenced the ideas and insights I have come to understand and share. Most significantly over the last couple of years, Patrick Walker, Ashleigh Armitage and the team from Dust who came up with the idea of Wayfinding and gave this book the theme that it previously lacked, as well as the often overlooked details that make for a more meaningful and enjoyable reading experience.

Foremost, of course, my Mum and Dad, who provided a sound, secure and solid basis for me to develop from. Then of course, my sister, brother, wife and more recently my daughters, who have challenged me and loved me, even when I failed. And everyone else I have encountered along the journey so far, whether I appreciated them at the time or not.

I have a profound debt of appreciation that I strive to repay in my work, for those people in various ways who have opened up and trusted me to work with them, to overcome troubling situations, and *live more happily. It is one thing to understand theoretically; it is another to apply that insight into a dynamic context in real time. Having seen the patterns in thousands of situations has helped me develop, discard, and reform the raw ideas that I held all those years ago when I began this wonderful journey.*

It was not just the problems and challenges that people brought to me, but also their own developed ideas, and I have been privileged to have merged a huge number of contrasting concepts together into a grander overview than I would ever have come up with alone. I truly believe that everyone holds a part of the puzzle, and when we can share honestly and freely and receive without prejudice, then we will all evolve so much faster, collectively and individually.

Special acknowledgement for the book you hold now must be made to Ruth Layton. Ruth and I first crossed paths when she was at a troubled point in her life and looking for answers. Thousands of other people have read the same book and many have told me that it was helpful to them. Yet I was too slow to take the hint that perhaps it should be pushed a little more and hid away to start all over again.

Ruth prodded me again and again to make this book more accessible and available, so that more people could benefit from its message. In the end, she took the time, effort, and investment to make this book more widely available because she cared so deeply for others in the same situation. And so you and I both owe Ruth for our meeting here.

Beyond this, Ruth is an exemplary model for anyone struggling with an issue or problem. As I often say, you can be right or you can be happy, but not both. At times in our communications, I was blunt and sometimes intentionally harsh in shattering some of Ruth's fondest aspirations. Yet never once did Ruth hide away from the truth or shrink from the pain. At times, it took time for her to let go of her most cherished wishes. But always, she remained steadfast to finding what was true, rather than what she wished was true.

It is this spirit of open-minded adventure of the Truth Seeker that Ruth exemplifies — that I hope you, too, will embrace as we journey through the challenges to your existing perspectives that are necessary for a strong foundation on which you can build a happy, peaceful, and adventurous life.

Thank you all for your companionship on this incredible journey of life.

WWW.
FIRSTFACE
NORTH.COM

Hi There

I hope you've enjoyed what you've just read and maybe now you're thinking so what now? Reading is a good start, yet it's what we do that changes us, and our lives, and that's why I want to be there on your journey for the next step. Like a Mad Scientist, it's my mission to constantly seek out truth and share what I find, so I'm always developing new ideas and ways to make living a happier life easier

For example, since writing this book I have shared many other tools, workbooks videos, reports, interviews and conversations such as;

The Zero Stress System

Happiness 2.0 Report

The Happiness Formula

The Self Audit, and much,
much more ...

Or you may be wondering one of
the questions that so many other
readers have asked and I've
answered, such as ...

Ok. That makes sense, but how
do I live it?

Why did you write the book?

Why are the stories printed in a
different direction?

Are the stories available in a
downloadable format?

I would love for you to join
me and fellow readers on this
journey, start discussions,
share your thoughts and ask
any questions. To join is easy,
just go to firstfacenorth.com

See you there! :)

Oh and one last thing, if you've
enjoyed this book I'd really
appreciate you writing a review
or Amazon. It's really important
in spreading the word and each
person that finds more personal
happiness leads to a happier
and more peaceful world.

Doesn't have to be anything too fancy, just what you got from the book and your experience of reading it. There's a link to the page at firstfacenorth.com

To your health and happiness,

R. McPhillips

www.firstfacenorth.com